The Rogue and the Wallflower

The Honorable Rogues®, Book Five

COLLETTE CAMERON

Blue Rose Romance®
Portland, Oregon

Sweet-to-Spicy Timeless Romance®

THE ROGUE AND THE WALLFLOWER
The Honorable Rogues®, Book Five
Copyright © 2017 Collette Cameron
Cover Design by: Darlene Albert

This book is a work of fiction. Names, characters, places, and incidents are the product of the author's imagination or are used fictitiously. Any resemblance to actual events, locales, or persons, living or dead, is coincidental.

All rights reserved under International and Pan-American Copyright Conventions. By downloading or purchasing a print copy of this book, you have been granted the non-exclusive, non-transferable right to access and read the text of this book. No part of this text may be reproduced, transmitted, downloaded, decompiled, reverse engineered, or stored in or introduced into any information storage and retrieval system, in any form or by any means, whether electronic or mechanical, now known or hereinafter invented without the express written permission of copyright owner.

Attn: Permissions Coordinator
Blue Rose Romance®
8420 N Ivanhoe # 83054
Portland, Oregon 97203

eBook ISBN: 9781954307476
Paperback ISBN: 9781954307483
www.collettecameron.com

"I've prayed for a man like you my whole life."
~Miss Shona Atterberry

"Beautiful chemistry...
You'll cheer for these star-crossed lovers."
Christi Gladwell USA Today Bestselling Author

The Honorable Rogues®
A Kiss for a Rogue
A Bride for a Rogue
A Rogue's Scandalous Wish
To Capture a Rogue's Heart
The Rogue and the Wallflower
A Rose for a Rogue

Check out Collette's Other Series
Castle Brides
Highland Heather Romancing a Scot
Daughters of Desire (Scandalous Ladies)
The Blue Rose Regency Romances:
The Culpepper Misses
Seductive Scoundrels
Heart of a Scot

Collections
Lords in Love
The Honorable Rogues® Books 1-3
The Honorable Rogues® Books 4-6
Seductive Scoundrels Series Books 1-3
Seductive Scoundrels Series Books 4-6
The Blue Rose Regency Romances-
The Culpepper Misses Series 1-2

Dedication

An author's most treasured gift—when a reader becomes a dear and beloved friend.

The Rogue and the Wallflower is for you Dee.

For all that you've done for me, for all of your unfailing support, for being a girly-girl like me, and most of all, for your precious friendship.

Love you bunches!

Collette

Acknowledgements

Firstly, I have to thank my VIP Reader Group, Collette's Cheris. When I run ideas past you, you give me honest and helpful feedback. I adore you!

The characters Aunt Barbara and Kandi are named after two of the group's members who won a contest. Thanks ladies, for the privilege, and I hope you enjoyed getting to know the characters I borrowed your names for.

Beta Babes, as always you came through for me. Your suggestions never fail to make my stories better. I appreciate the time you take to read, critique, edit, and share your opinions!

My most sincere gratitude to my assistants for all that you do so that I may write!

xoxo

Davenswood Court, Buckinghamshire

August 1819

A droplet of perspiration trickled between Shona's breasts leaving a dribbly, sticky trail despite her frantic fanning and the conservatory's open doors.

Would this summer's sweltering temperatures never cease?

How was she to appear dignified and fresh when moisture beaded every part of her person, from her brow to her toes tucked into quaint new turquoise slippers?

Desperate for relief, and despite the impropriety,

she'd removed her bonnet and gloves—who would know anyway? They, along with her parasol and the book she'd thought to read but abandoned, now lay atop a charming wrought iron bench situated beside the far door.

Cloying tendrils of hair stuck to her temples, and she feared her Indian sprigged muslin gown—chosen specifically for the fabric's airiness—exhibited humiliating damp spots in mortifying places.

Fingers spread, she held one hand beneath the miniature waterfall cascading from the upper level of the burbling fountain centered in the greenhouse. Even the water felt warm to her touch, and she would've forsaken shortbread for a month if she could stand beneath the Falls of Bruar's gushing flow at this very moment.

She patted her forehead and then her cheeks with her wet fingers.

The lush greenery and colorful flowers artfully displayed throughout Davenswood Court's hothouse, including a lemon and an orange tree, thrived in the tropical atmosphere.

Not so Shona. She wilted like a pansy plopped in freshly-poured oolong tea.

Selecting the most humid building on the estate to steal a few moments alone hadn't been the wisest of decisions. But even amidst this torrid heat, she relished the peace and privacy she'd filched by doing so.

Truth to tell, she'd also fled Miss Rossington and her two cohorts, the Dundercroft sisters. That trio of mean-spirited chits had been nothing but malicious since Shona had arrived yesterday.

Lacy fan splayed in her left hand, and lifting her skirts to a most indelicate height with her right, Shona ventured to the conservatory's other door. Once there, she covertly surveyed Davenswood Court's sprawling, neat-as-a-tailor's-seams lawns. She saw no one addlepated enough to attempt a stroll beneath the late-afternoon sun's punishing rays.

Excellent.

A bittersweet smile tipped her mouth. She wasn't ready to face the house party's growing throng just yet.

Never would, truth be told.

She was, to say the least, completely, hopelessly,

and chronically socially inept.

Oh, put her in a room with family members or close friends, and she produced the wittiest dialogue, the most intelligent, thought-provoking conversations. Even humorous ripostes. But amongst casual acquaintances or, worse yet, strangers?

Utterly hopeless.

A chair cushion or a teacup displayed more finesse and cleverness.

A wistful sigh escaped her as she eyed the sparkling indigo lake beyond the well-tended greens.

Bordered by a grove of towering, thickly-leafed, gnarly-branched oaks, the refreshing water beckoned. What she wouldn't give to strip her stockings and slippers from her sweaty legs and feet and soak her toes in the cool depths.

Out of the question, of course.

More's the pity.

Despite the heat, an icy shudder scythed across her shoulders.

Och. Just imagine the elevated brows, pinched mouths, and censured superior glances from the hoity-toity upper crust even now mingling within the manor house. The upper ten thousand weren't all pretentious and judgmental, of course. Regrettably, she seemed to be a magnet for those who were.

Hence, Shona had determined to remain as inconspicuous and innocuous as possible for the interminable seven days, eleven hours, and—she squinted at the blazing sun—however many torturous odd minutes remained before her zealously anticipated departure.

Too bad this wasn't Wedderford Abbey, her Scottish estate—her blessedly temperate, mild-weather home. There she could frolic about barefoot, gown hiked to her thighs, or swim naked as a robin if she wished.

Which, naturally, being a reserved and modest creature of twenty—*one-and-twenty tomorrow*—and possessing a title in her own right, she didn't.

Verra much. Verra often.

Last evening, several male guests—originally dismissing her as a frumpy, somewhat plump, beneath-their-touch Scot—became comically attentive and moon-eyed upon learning of her position and not-so-modest fortune. Worse than hunting hounds in full cry, once they'd caught the scent of her money and power.

A lady Lord of Parliament.

Shona had finally stopped trying to explain the complicated title to the cod-pated popinjays. She wished the Scots referred to the noble rank as a barony like the English did. So much simpler.

And why, for heaven's sake, couldn't whoever dreamed up the classification have created a feminine equivalent for women holding the rank?

Because in that, as in most things, men deem women irrelevant, incapable, or insignificant.

A movement caught her eye, and suddenly tense and alert, she swung her wary consideration toward the motion.

A tall man, his rather longish hair glinting with bronze streaks, strode with animal-like grace across the clipped lawn.

Headed straight for the lake, she'd be bound.

The stranger held one bare hand angled against his forehead, no doubt shading his eyes from the unrelenting sun. Still, his profile's silhouette revealed the sharp blade of a patrician nose, the slashing angle of high cheeks, and a sculpted chin.

A strong face. Ruggedly handsome. Arresting, in a sort of untamed, almost predatory way.

As he marched along, anger exuded from him in every stalking step of his powerful legs.

The fuggy air stalling in her lungs, like a doe in a hunter's sights, Shona stood stock still, fearful of detection.

Or so she told herself.

What other rational reason could there be for her breath to snag and her pulse to pitter-patter?

She was a sensible miss.

Not a totty-headed nincompoop given to histrionics, giggling, pouts, waterworks, swooning, or any other absurd feminine dramatics. No indeed. No coy twirling of parasols, fluttering of fans, artfully-dropped gloves. Good thing she had no inclination to flirt, for the artifice was so far beyond her scope, her maladroitness would bring further shame upon her.

Nevertheless, despite her complete and total lack

of feminine wiles, her dratted attention remained curiously—*disturbingly*—riveted on the gentleman.

His jacket's fabric strained against his biceps and shoulders, and with each long stride, the back of his coat hitched up, revealing what was surely one of the finest manly behinds she'd ever had the pleasure of observing.

Not that she made a regular habit of inspecting gentlemen's posteriors. Generally, when dashing men were near, she seldom lifted her focus from the floor or her slippers' toes.

She needn't have fretted he'd catch her staring, for not once did he glance her way.

His Spanish brown coat, biscuit-colored pantaloons, and ebony boots blended with the oaks' tawny-gray trunks, and in a few moments, he disappeared.

Suddenly, a touch cross and uncertain why, she muttered, "Too much to hope, I suppose, that the country air would be cooler than London." She fervently resumed waving her fan and gave her face a brisk cooling.

THE ROGUE AND THE WALLFLOWER

A much-coveted breeze wafted past, carrying the essence of several late-blooming flowers and vines. Her nostrils quivered, and she drew in an appreciative breath.

At least it smelled scads better here.

Town reeked most days. However, in the summer, the stench became intolerable. If required to venture outdoors, she often covered her nose with an orange-blossom scented handkerchief. She far preferred the fresh, invigorating air of the country—the Highlands in particular.

Wheels crunching on gravel drew her reluctant attention to the ostentatious mansion's circular drive. The portentous sound meant only one thing.

More guests for the Viscount and Viscountess Wimpletons' week-long house party.

An almost intractable, child-like frown pulled her brows together and turned her mouth downward.

Why did the Wimpletons have to be such gracious hosts and all-around nice people? Favorites amongst the upper echelons, to be sure.

Three dust-coated carriages rumbled to a stop, and

half a dozen maroon-and-black liveried footman rushed down the stairs to assist with the passengers' luggage.

Over sixty of Society's finest had descended on Davenswood Court already, and the party didn't officially commence until tomorrow and then concluded with a grand ball.

A masque ball, at that.

Such a wonderful, if somewhat small, reprieve.

A strip of satin across Shona's eyes would allay her discomfiture a touch, and was a trifle better than hovering in an alcove or hiding behind potted plants and vast columns. Or the humiliating awkwardness of sitting—overlooked and disregarded—with the other wallflowers and spinsterish misses. False smiles dredged from their pitiful reserve of pride couldn't conceal the hope warring with disappointment in their half-lowered gazes.

Despite a masque's welcome anonymity, she awaited the dance with the same enthusiasm as she might anticipate having a molar extracted or a carbuncle lanced. Not, mind you, that she'd ever experienced either. But Mama had, and she'd been a veritable bear for days before and afterward.

Mama is a crotchety, unreasonable, demanding bear all of the time.

Over one hundred guests, plus their servants, were expected, according to the maid helping Shona dress this morning.

For a week.

A whole, unbearably long, uncomfortable, angst-ridden, sure-to-make-a-cake-of-herself week. With the *haut ton's* elite members milling about, constantly underfoot, noting every little *faux pas* or gaffe. And likely not another peaceful, relaxed moment to herself until she reached Wedderford Abbey.

Depending on how many guests did, indeed, accept the invitation to the Wimpletons' much-coveted annual summer event, Shona might very well be obligated to share her assigned room with a stranger.

God help her if she found herself saddled with a chit of Miss Rossington's petulant ilk.

What a perfectly horrid notion.

Perhaps she could feign an illness?

No need to pretend. Shona swallowed the dread-induced queasiness throttling to her throat.

Why did she have to be such a coward?

Nae, not a coward.

Just wretchedly cow-handed and fearful of making social blunders. Which she did with astonishing regularity and generally humiliating results.

Chagrin-born flames licked her face.

Perfect.

Now her round cheeks even more resembled two ripe, *riddy* apples.

Stepping through the doorway, mindful to remain within the building's shade lest the sun reach her easily-freckled skin, she worried her lower lip. How she wished to escape to the lake for the rest of the afternoon.

Probably some social rule against unaccompanied, unmarried females wandering the estate. Until such a female was soundly on the shelf, and then the restrictions were eased a smidge.

Not enough to suit her, by thunder and turf.

Most people thought her an insipid milk-and-water

miss, which wasn't accurate in the least. But neither was she a piss-and-vinegar chit either. She actually possessed a rather vibrant spirit—a verve she studiously kept subdued beneath her bashful mannerisms. But nothing so forward or unacceptable as actual brazenness, or—

What was that colorful expression she'd overheard the stable hand mutter last week? Nose scrunched, she shut her eyes.

Ah, that was it.

The cheeky boldness of a bloke with bull-sized ballocks.

Oh, to be able to claim the merest jot of such incontestable confidence. Not the ballocks part, of course. Just the boldness.

Years of maternal abuse had turned Shona into a timorous mouse of a thing, and she hated it. Loathed being a dowdy, bashful, gaffe-prone wallflower. Just once, she'd like to hold her head high, poised and self-assured.

Once, dare something a trifle wicked or wanton.

Or both.

Her nape hairs prickled a warning, and she darted an uneasy peek over her shoulder.

No one approached the greenhouse.

Must she be so jumpy, for pity's sake?

Her errant focus glided back to the lake. If only she possessed the nerve to test the inviting water. But such rash action would bring censure on those she cared for.

If she had an ounce of steel in her, she'd use this house party to her advantage. Perhaps even get herself kissed for the first time. *Oooh. At the masque ball.* Or better yet, set her cap, her handkerchief—by heavens, her parasol and gloves too—for a gentleman she found striking.

And kind.

He must be kind. And patient. And not given to raising his voice or poking fun at her weight or figure.

She'd had a lifetime of being lectured and screeched at, and too many biscuits, sweet meats, and pastries as a child had developed into excess curves she couldn't seem to rid herself of no matter how many reducing diets she tried, food choices she restricted, or lengthy daily walks she took.

Even the multiple occasions when Mother had locked her in her room for days with scarcely anything to eat hadn't willowed her form.

Shona's mouth twitched on one side.

Likely due to her figuring out how to pick the lock and helping herself to whatever she pleased from the kitchen. Much to Cook and Mama's consternation. Neither could fathom where the food disappeared to, but never knowing when Mama would choose to deprive her of meals again, Shona always wrapped a supply to stash in her chamber.

Her dearest friend, Katrina, the Duchess of Pendergast, had tried to convince Shona that she wasn't prone to plumpness.

Pooh. What benevolent drivel.

The looking glass Shona peered into every day didn't lie. Her bosoms were ... well ... *big*. And her hips flared out, generous and full, from her waist.

She formed a small pout with her mouth.

Och. To have slender, narrow hips and thighs. What a lovely thing that would be.

True, no flabby flesh jiggled about beneath her chemise, but at soirée after rout after assembly—when she'd braved lifting her gaze from her hands neatly clasped in her lap—she'd witnessed gentlemen flocking to the lithe, svelte misses. Or the full-bosomed ones with willowy hips, while chuffy, unexceptional lasses such as herself were seldom spared a second glance.

"I'm positive I saw our Lady Atterberry slip out the terrace doors, Clarence, dear."

Velma Olson.

A familiar grating voice penetrated Shona's turbulent musings.

Hangnails and hoary toads.

From behind a potted palm, which did little to conceal her, Shona peeked through the other door. A frustrated groan escaped her pursed mouth.

Confound it. She'd been discovered.

Beneath a purple-fringed parasol, Clarence Olson and his domineering mother tramped toward the conservatory, red-faced and perspiring like lathered racehorses.

"And when she did, I purposed to find you at once," Mrs. Olson said. "It's providence, surely. She'll welcome your addresses, darling. How could she not? You're third in line to a viscountcy." Pomposity dripped from each affected word. "Trust me. Mothers know these things."

What colossal windbaggery.

Shona wouldn't have had Clarence Olson if the peacocks wandering the estate started singing opera. In Gaelic.

Jaw set, she folded her fan and reached into the hothouse to drop it onto the bench with her other belongings. If the Olsons thought she was ripe for the plucking, they'd find themselves gravely mistaken.

"I believe I saw movement near the greenhouse." Slightly breathless, Mrs. Olson rattled on, "Surely a bashful Scots drab such as she realizes the honor you bestow on her with your attention."

"Hardly a drab, Mother," Mr. Olson denied with an impatient shake of his sandy blond-haired head. "She's really most comely, and I find her accent quite charming."

Shona barely stifled a derisive snort.

Comely? Charming?

Been nipping his flask of brandy a bit early today, had he?

She wasn't in the mood for those two.

Like dogs trailing a fox, they'd pursued her relentlessly since Lady Wimpleton had introduced them.

Shona was no fool.

Neither Mrs. Olson nor her bird-witted fop of a son had given her a second look until someone addressed her as Lady Atterberry. Then at once, the rapacious pair had openly questioned several guests about her status. Suddenly, they'd became as attentive as miserly bankers counting their hoarded bank notes.

Fisting her skirts, Shona lifted them scandalously high, exposing the entirety of her calves, and tore from the greenhouse as if hell's hounds nipped at her satin-covered heels. She'd have preferred the devil's own dogs to the Olsons' importuning presences.

The oak grove wasn't so very far away, and the chance of someone else seeing her pelting, neck or nothing, was slight. She hoped.

"Lady Atterberry. Wait."

Mrs. Olson's shrill voice raked down Shona's spine, like a freshly-honed gardening claw.

I think not.

Breathless from her charge across the grass, her lovely slippers hopelessly stained, Shona plowed into the oaks' delicious shade. Glorious coolness engulfed her. Despite her frantic flight, she sighed in appreciation. This was where she ought to have hidden away. Next time—

"Lady Atterberry?" Mr. Olson's reedy voice rang far too near. "Where'd the gel git to?"

"She's in the trees, of course," Mrs. Olson said, peevishness sharpening her voice.

Tossing a frantic glance over her shoulder—the dratted pair were still hell-bent on finding her—Shona stumbled over a massive root snaking across the ground.

A wee squeal escaped her. Arms flailing, she fought to regain her balance. From the corner of her eye, she saw the man in brown sprinting toward her, his hands outstretched.

The instant before she plummeted headfirst into the lake, her gaze met his piercing, sky-blue eye.

2

Ankles crossed, Morgan lounged against a thick trunk. An oak cluster had grown together, creating a natural alcove, even forming a crude seat.

Still seething from another ugly encounter with Father, which had left him feeling betrayed as well as enraged, he randomly skipped rocks across the lake's gleaming surface. Sending the flat stones flying released a modicum of the tension throttling through his veins.

He heard the woman's boisterous entry into this, his coveted sanctuary, before he saw her. Her tiny yelp alerted him, and he wheeled toward her.

Too late.

Her rosebud mouth parted into a startled 'O'. Her

wide, doe-like eyes, the color of warm caramel and filled with shock, embarrassment, and horror, latched onto his.

He lengthened his stride, lurching for her with outstretched hands.

An instant later, her very shapely calves disappeared over a steep drop-off.

Without hesitation, he shucked his coat and tore off his neckcloth. No time to remove his boots, dammit. And they were new too. A pity gift from his sister Viola.

Those unfamiliar with the terrain didn't realize that, though the ground appeared level, a steep precipice dropped straight into the lake.

Poised on the overhang, he searched the depths for the woman.

There.

A beleaguered head bobbed to the surface. Mouth open, she panted, scraggly locks of sable hair covering most of her face.

Did she know how to swim?

Even if she did, she'd struggle to make it to shore

with her skirts wrapped about her legs

In one swift, smooth movement, Morgan dove into the water. If he hadn't been holding his breath, he would've gasped. To his overheated body, the freezing cold came as a shock and a blessing.

Surfacing, he treaded water, trying to locate her.

As yet unaware of his presence, she bobbed several yards away, barely keeping her head above the water. Her expression determined, her movements labored, she started for shore.

Devil it.

As Morgan suspected, her skirts hampered her, weighing her down like great sodden sails.

What if he hadn't been here?

She would've drowned for certain. Still might.

The black thought burrowed deep in his chest, causing a queer tightness where it anchored.

After dragging in a lungful of air, Morgan hollered. "Turn onto your back and float until I get there."

Eyes round with shock, she jerked her dark head his way.

Profound relief flooded her pretty features. Obediently, she rotated onto her back, her breasts—the bodice stuck to the full orbs like a second skin—jutted above the water line, the ends pebbled from cold.

He swept a fleeting, appreciative gaze over the mounds.

Voluptuous figures had always attracted him.

Tend to the task at hand, Le Draco. The gel needn't drown while you ogle her marvelous charms.

With swift, strong strokes, he swam to her. He'd regained most of his strength after the explosion–something that had seemed impossible in the early days of his convalescence. Other than several hideous scars, reduced hearing in his left ear, and the loss of an eye, he was restored.

Physically.

His highly-coveted position in the 1st Royal Regiment of Dragoons, on the other hand…

Fortune hadn't smiled on him in that regard.

While he'd been unconscious and no one had known whether he'd live or die, his sire had taken it upon himself to retire Morgan's commission.

Now at eight-and-twenty, he had nothing to go back to.

Nothing to look forward to.

No purpose. No direction. No rudder to steer his life and guide him.

Unless—*until*—he found employment. He'd become a societal parasite, dependent on the goodwill and generosity of his friends and sister, for he refused to accept a guinea from his father, Ruben Le Draco.

Damned lucky to have survived.

So Morgan had been told over and over.

And over.

The blast had killed five, maiming and wounding dozens more, but he—

Stow it.

As he approached, the girl turned her head. The gratitude in her expression transformed to incredulity when she spied his eyepatch and the vicious scar's jagged path to his mouth, pulling one corner up at a grotesque angle.

After a year, he ought to have been accustomed to the stunned reactions. Yet, he still cringed inwardly when people—women, especially—flinched and gasped or hastily averted their gazes.

And when children's faces crumpled in terror—

Enough.

But this profoundly unique creature didn't look away. Instead, her attention shifted to his remaining eye, and such sympathy blossomed on her porcelain face that his thrumming heart battered against its bruised walls.

Struggling to stay afloat, she managed a timorous smile, full of kindness and empathy.

In that instant, through some sort of preternatural instinct, Morgan knew she'd suffered too. Here she was, her pulse raging at the base of her delicate throat, in very real danger of drowning, and instead of turning away in disgust or revulsion, she'd shown him compassion.

Where the hell would she go, man? It's not like she has any choice at present.

"Don't be alarmed, but in order to help you ashore, I must put my arm around your middle."

Teeth chattering, a bluish tint around the edges of

her lips, she gave a shaky nod.

From behind, Morgan encircled her torso, and she stifled a gasp. The plump pillows of her bosoms lay heavily on his forearm. He couldn't help but admire their fullness. Another time, he might have more completely appreciated the tantalizing display.

"Lay your head against my shoulder," he gently ordered.

Crimping her mouth into a prim line, she nodded again then dutifully rested her soggy head on his shoulder. Her quaking vibrated his chest.

Fear as much as cold, he'd be bound.

For reasons he couldn't begin to gauge, reassuring her was vital. He spoke softly into her ear. "It's all right. I have you now. I promise, you'll be in your chamber enjoying a hot bath within the half hour."

A shuddery sigh escaped through her parted lips, and she relaxed against him.

Probably oughtn't to have mentioned a bath, for now he couldn't tear his focus from her breasts and stop envisaging bathwater, liberally dosed with scented oil, lapping the rounded mounds. Teasing the rosy tips into hard nubs.

He drew in a long breath, as much from physical exertion as to enjoy her heady scent.

She smelled sweet and delicate. Orange blossoms, but also something musky and a mite earthier.

"Should I kick? I think I can if I pull my gown up." Her voice was low and languid around the edges, as if she struggled to speak.

Did he detect the faintest trace of a Scottish brogue?

"If you're able to, yes. That would help."

Enormously.

This was no skinny miss, all sharp angles and bony contours. Her shapely form deserved further consideration and admiration. But on dry land, when such pleasant contemplation didn't put them at risk of ending up on the lake bottom.

And with his waterlogged boots, getting them to shore was proving a considerable task.

"I've certainly given the guests something to prattle about," she quipped, raising her gaze, warm and sweet as dark honey, to study him above her forehead.

In a bungling, unpolished sort of way, her attempt at levity was heartwarming.

"Indeed."

He winked, and her pansy eyes rounded, delicate color flaring across her cheekbones.

They couldn't go ashore where she'd tumbled into the lake, so he guided them to another area of the beach.

Olson and his annoying, always-looking-down-her-superior-than-thou-nose mother stood gawking nearby, their unhinged jaws drooping to their knobby knees. Denton Olson, however, was notably absent.

No surprise there.

Likely the elder Olson had eschewed the house party and his wife's and son's *titillating* company. Perfect opportunity for him to spend a week in the cozy cottage he'd set his current mistress up in.

A few minutes later—probably no more than three or four, but to Morgan's burning lungs and fatigued muscles, it felt like hours—he hauled the young woman into shallow water.

Breathing raggedly, he managed to prop her up,

and after scrambling to his feet, offered her his hand.

"Here," he gasped. "Permit me to help you stand."

Even bedraggled and soggy, and with her hair plastered to her face, her soft treacle eyes glowed with gratitude, and another rosy blush swept up her cheeks' gentle slopes.

Who was she?

Not one of the usual country house party set, to be sure.

Neither Olson made an effort to assist them. Probably afraid of getting their clothes wet or muddy.

However, Clarence Olson did concede to greet Morgan with a grudging, somewhat curt nod. "Dragon."

Morgan clenched his jaw, his nails cutting into his palms.

Steady on.

He sucked in a silent, calming breath, forcing himself to relax and smile casually, as if unaffected by the deliberate slur. "Le Draco will do, Olson."

Leave it to that sod to call Morgan by the nickname his regiment had bestowed upon him after the Battle of Waterloo. Few dared voice it to his face, and he'd bet his ruined boots the knave had done so to blacken his character to the woman shivering before them.

"Olson, I tossed my coat aside over there." Morgan pointed in the general vicinity of where he'd heaved the garment. "Fetch it. Please. She's freezing."

Not for long. In this scorching heat, her gown would dry in minutes.

For an instant, Morgan thought he'd refuse, but after his mother touched his arm and murmured something, Olson gave a terse nod and trudged off in the direction Morgan had indicated.

Hugging herself, her chin tucked to her chest, the woman sloshed to shore. Her gown clung just as tenaciously to her backside, giving Morgan a glimpse of wondrously plump buttocks.

A heady wave of lust engulfed him, and he balled his hands against the urge to graze his palm over the supple mounds.

Since the accident, he hadn't enjoyed feminine delights. No women besides trollops, and deuced few of them, welcomed a disfigured, half-blind man into their beds. And even had he ever been inclined to dally with trulls, he hadn't the coin to spare.

Olson approaching with Morgan's coat prevented him from making a complete arse of himself. He wrenched his befuddled gaze away from her delectable behind and swiped his hair off his forehead, shoving the longer-than-fashionable strands behind his ears.

A mocking grin twitched his mouth.

He really ought to get his hair cut. But his long locks irritated Father so much, Morgan had refused to let scissors near his head since learning his sire had overstepped the bounds and taken it upon himself to make the life-changing decision to terminate Morgan's military career.

His refusal to enter the family business riled Ruben Le Draco more than Morgan's overly long hair. Every time Morgan saw Father, his sire toddled down the same contentious, verbally plowed-to-bedrock path.

"As a dutiful son, Morgan, you're obligated to oversee the sugar plantations and refineries."

Why? So his avaricious father might grow wealthier at the expense of the wretched, abused slaves sweating their lives away in the tropics?

No, by God. Morgan wasn't having any of it. Ever. He might not have much left in the way of pride or dignity, but his integrity and honor remained intact.

He'd told Ruben as much. Again. Not more than a half hour ago. Nothing this side of heaven or hell would ever compel him to profit off the suffering of others.

Playing the gallant and holding Morgan's jacket open, Olson's contorted his mouth into an oily, sycophantic smile. "Allow me, Lady Atterberry."

Lady Atterberry?

Married then.

Morgan's ribcage tightened. He had no right to feel such a fulminating crest of disappointment, like a rusty knife twisting in his gut.

Olson draped Morgan's jacket over Lady Atterberry's quivering shoulders. Had he been a true gentleman, he'd have offered his own coat, since Morgan stood dripping into his boots.

"Thank you." She kept her attention fixed on her muddy, once white stocking-clad toes, her shred of a voice so soft, Morgan barely heard her.

Something akin to jealousy gripped him that his coat should have the pleasure of touching her when he could not.

"You disappeared right after breakfast." The corners of Olson's mouth sidled upward in what he no doubt believed was a charming smile.

Looked more like a rat about to pounce on a fresh, flaky croissant a baker had accidentally dropped.

No. Make that a posturing rooster.

Chest puffed out, one knee bent, and a hand resting upon his hip, he stood as if posed for a portrait. Temptation sorely prodded Morgan to inquire if Olson expected a portraitist forthwith.

"You missed a rousing croquet tournament," Olson said, still postured in his ridiculous stance.

Rousing?

Racing a horse neck or nothing across the Scottish moors was rousing.

Surviving a bloody battle when your troops were

outnumbered was rousing.

Even a quadrille with a certain pretty, sable-haired damsel with compelling melted chocolate eyes might be considered rousing.

Arousing, to be sure.

However, the only thing croquet could ever be credited with stimulating was wide yawns. And only a complete boor would've introduced the topic on the cusp of a near drowning with the victim still shivering from terror and cold.

"Croquet holds little fascination for me, I'm afraid, Mr. Olson." The pale honey of Lady Atterberry's skin glowed in the sunbeams sifting through the foliage above. Her voice had gained strength, and she gave Morgan a direct, if somewhat hesitant, look. "My interests lie in other areas."

A double *entendre*?

Surely Morgan had imagined it.

Nonetheless, his cynical heart jostled a trifle giddily behind his ribs. Then kicked into a rousing— *yes, rousing*—triumphant jig when Olson's faced hardened, aggravation bracketing his mouth.

"My lady, I'm certain we can find a pastime we'd both enjoy," Olson persisted.

Doubtful she's fond of drinking, gaming, or whoring.

"Archery?" he inquired hopefully.

"No. I fear not." She shoved sopping strands of hair off her cheeks. "I never learned the skill."

"Lawn bowling? Shuttlecock? Riding?"

Desperation raised Olson's voice to a near whine when she shook her head after each suggestion. He cut his mother a fraught glance, to which she screwed her mouth and eyes tight, her expression shrieking, *Try harder, dolt.*

"Whist or loo? Charades? Singing? Canoeing? Fishing?"

Good God. Fishing?

Lady Atterberry's adorable turned-up nose crinkled the tiniest bit. "No. I don't fish. In fact, fish makes me ill."

Morgan just managed to check his gleeful guffaw.

Oh, poorly done, Olson. Very poorly done. Made a grand impression there.

THE ROGUE AND THE WALLFLOWER

Everyone knew the Olsons were on the prowl for an heiress and in dun territory up to their haughty eyebrows. Almost as bad as Morgan's own purse-pinched pockets. Except, unlike Olson, he'd never pursue a woman for her money. And neither was he third in line for a title.

Why all this posturing for Lady Atterberry if she was married, then? It didn't make any sense. Perhaps she'd been widowed. Awfully young to have suffered that travesty.

Unless she'd married an ancient codger.

A droplet of water teased a slow path down Morgan's forehead, and he swiped it away.

Imagining a decrepitude codger's cold gnarly fingers caressing her tender flesh left an acrid taste in his mouth. He swallowed and, eyes narrowed in censure, stared pointedly at Olson's hands.

They remained cupped upon Lady Atterberry's milky shoulders.

Morgan set his jaw against an insane urge to wrench the dandy's sweaty palms off her. And then toss the twiddlepoop into the lake. That ought to cool the ardor glinting in Olson's randy gaze.

Instead, wringing out his shirttail, Morgan studiously, leisurely, and most thoroughly, took her measure.

He refused to ponder why exactly, other than her curvaceous form could tempt a saint. Which he assuredly was not.

Why did he feel so protective then? Possessive even?

Hers wasn't the first life he'd saved, and there wasn't anything heroic about diving into the lake. He'd only acted the gentleman. Done what any decent chap would've done. And in all honestly, he hadn't been positive he was equal to the task. Those last few feet had been murderous.

He slanted a dubious brow at Olson.

Morgan doubted that unprincipled jackanape would've risked his life to save her, even had she been his wife. Olson couldn't even be bothered to help her ashore after Morgan had plopped her in the shallows.

And Olson seriously thought she'd welcome his attentions after that oversight?

His noggin must be as dense as the oaks surrounding them.

"My dear young lady, Clarence will escort you back to the manor," Mrs. Olson declared, her pointy nose angled authoritatively. "I must admit, I cannot conceive how you found yourself in the lake."

"I clumsily tripped on a root and fell in." Lady Atterberry hadn't even attempted to alter the truth or paint herself in a more favorable light.

However, such self-castigation riddled her voice that Morgan longed to reassure her.

Mrs. Olson cut the sparkling water a dubious look before glancing at Morgan's face. Unable to completely conceal her distaste, her artificial smile wobbled, and her attention skittered away. "So very fortunate Captain Le Draco was nearby."

"Yes. It was. Most fortunate, indeed." Lady Atterberry tilted her head at a winsome angle. Shyly peeking at him from beneath her thick, spiky lashes—looking like a soaking-wet kitten—she offered Morgan what he suspected was a rare, genuine smile.

Her innocent gaze softened at the corners as she

regarded him. Warm and sincere, her mesmerizing, chocolatey eyes sucked him in. Nothing coy or pretentious about Lady Atterberry. A true original.

He rather liked that. Liked it a great deal, in truth. And he hadn't any right to. He'd nothing—absolutely nothing—to offer any woman.

Getting miles ahead of yourself there, old chap. Rein in your cavorting imagination.

"I must thank you, Captain. I'm not convinced I'd have made it ashore without your assistance. Please forgive my ineptness, which compelled you to jump in after me." The slope of Lady Atterberry's cheeks pinkened charmingly again. Her regard sank to his sodden boots, and her forehead furrowed into two neat rows. "Your boots are quite ruined. You must allow me to replace them."

Her contrite gaze met his before fluttering over his shoulders and hips, then flitting away like a nervous little bird.

His groin constricted at her timid perusal. What was it about this woman that penetrated the surface of his emotions and stirred his dormant senses to full alert? Dangerous that, and not a path he dared venture along.

"And your garments too, naturally." Embarrassment, or perhaps strain, made her speech clipped and formal, yet an undercurrent of sensual awareness tinged it too.

"That's not necessary." He hadn't sunk so low as to accept clothing from damsels he'd rescued. For the party's duration, he could always borrow boots from his closest chum, Allen Wimpleton. They were of the same size and build. "You are well worth the sacrifice."

Faint color flared across Lady Atterberry's cheeks once more.

"Come along at once, dear girl. You don't want to catch a chill. Clarence, take her arm." Clearly not pleased with the conversation's turn, or perhaps sensing Morgan's budding fascination, Mrs. Olson flapped her hand between her son and Lady Atterberry. "I shall brook no refusal."

What a controlling, interfering harridan she'd be as a mother-in-law. God spare Lady Atterberry that purgatory.

Before Olson could grasp her elbow, Lady Atterberry scooted away, her discomfiture as obvious as her soaked appearance. She caught her lower lip between her small, white teeth, then, with apparent resolve, straightened her spine, raised her head, and notched her delicate chin upward.

Admiration swelled in Morgan's chest.

Well done you, Lady Atterberry.

Her frank gaze sought his, a question, or perhaps a plea, in its glowing depths. "Thank you for your kind offer. However, there's no need. The captain already graciously offered to see me safely to the house."

3

Where Shona marshalled the courage to spout such outlandish flummery, she couldn't begin to venture.

But it felt wonderful.

So wonderful in fact, that in that instant, she determined to do so again.

And again. And again.

Not tell thumpers, just speak her mind and do as she wanted more often.

Captain Le Draco's mouth slid into an approving smile, his azure eye, the tiny flecks of silver there, flashing with wry amusement.

His support bolstered her growing courage.

"I did indeed promise." Humor infused his

melodic baritone. With a smart bow, all proper decorum and politesse, he extended his right arm as if she were a princess he escorted to The Theatre Royale.

A giggle almost escaped Shona at the vinegary expressions pleating the Olsons' faces and cinching their prune-like puckered mouths. The darkling look Mrs. Olson glowered at the captain nearly caused another round of uncontrolled mirth.

Only by biting the inside of her cheek was she able to check her jollity.

If she'd offered them sugared earthworms or glazed maggots during tea, they couldn't have appeared more offended. Yet, how could they raise a breeze? As new acquaintances, they held no power over her and certainly had no right to any expectations.

Perceptibly displeased with the situation, they exchanged a peeved, telling glance.

Good.

Perhaps they'd take the hint and leave off their pursuit. She'd never allow a gentleman of Mr. Olson's weak character to pay his addresses. And a more disagreeable mother-in-law she couldn't envisage.

Far better to remain unwed.

Shona darted an uncertain look upward to find the captain observing her with that same grave contemplation he'd regarded her with earlier.

What was he thinking?

Did he find her inadequate too?

The thought chinked away at her burgeoning confidence like rust relentlessly eroding iron. She almost retreated into her customary shell of silence and fled to the house. However, the kindness tempering the hard lines of his face and warming the edges of his eyes encouraged her.

Shona trailed a sympathetic visual path over the scar slashing his face's left side.

What on Earth had happened to him?

How horribly painful it must've been, unfortunate man. She'd half raised her fingers to her cheek in sympathy before she caught herself.

Others might think him *hackit* and unpleasant to look upon. She couldn't have disagreed more.

Nae, nothing about his countenance was ugly.

The strong angles and planes of his face still

modeled a proud if somewhat harsh masculine beauty she found hard to ignore. Much the same way a damaged Grecian or Roman sculpture remained timelessly breathtaking despite its obvious imperfections. One didn't focus one's attention on what was missing or marred, but rather admired the undeniable awe-inspiring magnificence that had endured.

"You needn't wait for the captain and me. I've lost my slippers, so my progress will be considerably slower than yours." Shona offered the Olsons a genial smile to lessen the sting of her words.

My, but she'd grown bold as polished brass buttons since making the captain's acquaintance mere minutes ago. And what an utterly lovely, heady feeling. She could get rather accustomed to this. In the past five minutes, she'd demonstrated more gumption than...

Well, ever in her memory.

Perhaps not terribly audacious by some standards, but certainly an acceptable beginning for a diffident mouse of a thing.

THE ROGUE AND THE WALLFLOWER

Clutching Captain Le Draco's coat closed across her bosoms with one hand, she looped the other through his extended elbow. The merest hint of cologne wafted up from his jacket. A clean, manly aroma. Faintly spicy. Woodsy, even.

At once comforting and invigorating.

Neither of the Olsons moved an inch.

Not even when a bird flitting about the oak's branches pooped on Mr. Olson's shoulder.

Shona choked on another restrained laugh and faked a cough into her cupped palm when Mrs. Olson's eyes narrowed in suspicion.

Evidently Captain Le Draco had no such compunction for he laughed outright, despite Mr. Olson's denigrating glare.

His mother opened her mouth, no doubt to object to Shona's suggestion, but before she uttered a syllable, Captain Le Draco smoothly suggested, "If you would be so kind as to hurry ahead, find our hostess, and inform her that Lady Atterberry requires a bath drawn straightaway. I'd advise hot tea and broth too. For as you sagely advised, Mrs. Olson, we wouldn't want her ladyship taking a chill."

Oh, my.

The captain possessed the cheeky boldness of a bloke with bull-sized ballocks.

Rampant heat streaked to Shona's hairline even as her focus gravitated to *that* part of his anatomy.

"As you say," Mrs. Olson ground out as if chewing glass. Her gray eyes sinking into irritated slits, the irises barely visible between her lids, she gave a terse nod. No match for the captain, she evidently knew when she'd been beaten. "We shall see you at dinner, Lady Atterberry. It's *my* fervent wish that afterward you'll permit Clarence a turn about the terrace or gardens with you on his arm. And of course, you must save him a waltz at the ball."

Not a polite request but the command of a domineering woman accustomed to getting her own way.

Then you're in for a disappointment, my dear lady. I do not waltz.

She must've read the refusal in Shona's bland stare.

With a curt jut of her chin, Mrs. Olson grabbed her son's arm and all but dragged him across the lawn.

A scowl marring his handsome face, he glanced behind him, his perturbed gaze waffling between Shona and Captain Le Draco. His expression fairly shouted, "How can she favor *him* over me?"

Shona stepped nearer the captain, sending a silent, but unmistakable message.

She did prefer this scarred, disfigured man to Mr. Olson's carefully polished good looks. She'd choose sound character over practiced charm any day.

"I feared she wasn't going to take the hint, and I'd have to resort to impoliteness." The captain chuckled, a deep, pleasant rumble behind his ribs that drew Shona's attention to the dark, curly mat of hair his parted collar revealed.

Her insides turned soft and malleable, while her pulse ticked up a notch.

How could a man she'd just met have such a profound effect? Was she, who couldn't flirt and was a pathetic disaster at womanly wiles, all aflutter?

"As did I. Since yester eve, they've been quite

persistent and annoying." Dash it. Why had she said that? Now he'd think her a gossip or an unkind shrew.

"How so?" Considerate of her shoeless feet, Captain Le Draco took small strides and guided her around any debris on the ground.

A songbird chirruped overhead, and she automatically sought the source. A little bird with a blueish-brown head hopped along a branch, watching their progress.

As they sauntered along, the captain's coat brushed her thighs. Shona absently rubbed the jacket's fabric between her forefinger and thumb while contemplating her response.

Should she tell him her reservations about the Olsons? Would he think her shallow or conceited and full of self-importance? Worse yet, what if Captain Le Draco was, indeed, another opportunist? A roué?

Well, even if he turned out to be a full-on knave, he'd risked his life to save hers. She truly didn't think she'd have been able to swim to shore. The beach was inaccessible from where she'd toppled into the lake, and with her water-logged garments, the stretch to where he'd bundled her aground would've been too far for her to swim.

Her impulsive, imprudent flight might've ended her life. Better she face her adversary next time.

At the very least, she owed Captain Le Draco a brief explanation.

"Last evening, the Olsons learned that I possess a title, along with an endowment."

There. Captain Le Draco would either prove himself a charlatan like the others—*Oh, don't let it be so*, her timid heart cried—or, he'd turn out to be the caliber of man she suspected he was.

Hoped he was. Needed him to be.

"Ah." A smile skewed his mouth, his scar hitching his lips up farther on one side.

"Besides, I don't waltz. It is a dance for graceful women. Women light on their feet." Which she was not. She knew how to, of course. Mama had insisted she learn. The harsh truth was, Shona had never been asked to partner a man for the dance.

"You've yet to find the right partner then." He gave her a rather bashful look. "Might I be so bold as to request you reserve one for me?"

She wanted to say yes, but dared not. For his sake. "I've never attempted a waltz in public. I'm afraid I'd make a hash of the steps. Tromp your toes. Trip over my gown."

Or something equally inept and mortifying.

"Then we'll practice together beforehand. We've almost a week." He gave her a roguish wink and canted his head. "I've been told, I make a fair partner."

With his eye patch and flowing hair, it gave him a rakish swashbuckler appearance. All he needed was a saber belted at his waist, a crimson scarf across his forehead, and a golden loop shining from one ear. Wholly charming and irresistible to imaginative bluestocking misses more accustomed to being snubbed than admired.

He was the stuff of which romantic legends were woven.

She couldn't resist his offer. "All right. I suppose we might practice in the conservatory."

"Perfect."

She enjoyed the sensation of his firm muscles

flexing beneath her fingers too much. Even more, she'd reveled in his arm snugly embracing her, holding her tight against his sculpted, muscled shoulder as he towed her to shore. Never had she been as aware of a man in her life. But then again, no man had ever held her so intimately either.

And the captain was a big man.

So large she didn't feel all that cumbersome and ungraceful with him near. In fact—could it be true?—she felt feminine, and if not petite, at least delicate beside his towering, solidly-muscled form. Muscles which bulged and rippled beneath his damp shirt quite divinely as he walked.

Heavens. Since when did she notice men's muscles?

You noticed his bum earlier.

It took every iota of self-control Shona possessed not to sneak another look at that particular portion of his anatomy.

Captain Le Draco pressed her hand to his arm, the gesture so natural, she couldn't ponder the inappropriateness. "When I heard you addressed as

Lady Atterberry, I confess, I feared you were married."

He inclined his sable head, his regard dropping to her mouth before gravitating back to her eyes. Something intense and commanding flashed in his.

She tamped down the most insane desire to lick her lips.

Wait—

He *feared* she was married?

He feared I was married?

Feared?

In her mind, she chanted the lovely phrase, trying to decipher his precise meaning.

Was it too much to hope he was glad she wasn't?

Of course, a fortune-hunter would be relieved, her skeptical conscience jeered.

Captain Le Draco pushed a hank of hair behind his ear that had fallen forward, and as if he were nervous, cleared his throat.

She found the boyish act endearing and a startling contrast to the battle-hardened soldier who'd earned the moniker Dragon. Even she, as sheltered as she'd been, had heard whispers about the young cavalryman who'd single-handedly slain ten—a dozen or more if one listened to the exaggerated tales—French soldiers at Waterloo.

"Lady Atterberry, I suppose I ought to properly introduce myself since neither of the Olsons thought to do so. I know it's not quite *de rigueur,* but I'm sure you're as curious as I. And I won't tell anyone we breached decorum if you won't."

He inclined his head in that sleek mannish way she'd already come to associate with him.

"Captain Morgan Reed Kincaid Le Draco, formerly of the 1st Royal Regiment of Dragoons."

She dipped into a fairly graceful curtsy—wobbling only a little, she proudly noted. "Shona Beatrice Imelda Atterberry. Or, I suppose, if properly done, Shona, Lady Atterberry. I inherited a Scottish Lord of Parliament title."

"I'm deeply honored, my lady." One hand at his waist—a purplish, convoluted scar zig-zagging from his wrist to his middle finger, he bowed. "That's the equivalent of an English barony, isn't it?" he said as he straightened, then took her elbow once more.

The captain's touch sent another of those wondrous tremors skidding over her flesh. She seemed all tingly nerves and prickly sensations around him. Attuned to the largeness of his presence in a feminine way she'd never experienced with any man.

She gave him a delighted smile, inordinately pleased he knew that trivial detail. "Yes. It causes a bit of confusion at times."

"That explains your almost indiscernible brogue. It's just barely apparent when you're distressed or excited."

Despite Mother's efforts to beat the accent out of me.

How astute of him to notice. None other than he had ever commented on it. He was inordinately observant. Must be his soldier's training.

"Are you here with your family, Lady Atterberry?"

True interest? Banal conversation? Or did he fish for details?

Och, Shona. Ye've become as suspicious as Mama.

He might as well know the truth of it.

She'd already experienced a degree of censure as a result of her mother's sordid crimes. However, the blades and young bloods seeking a wealthy wife didn't seem to mind her tainted past all that much. Money and position covered a multitude of sins, it seemed.

"No, Captain. I came with Bridget and Hugh Needham." She slid him a sidelong look and discovered he closely observed her. Normally, that would have her blushing, stumbling and stuttering over her words. Where was her usual timorousness? "I've lived with them for the past two years."

That she could speak freely and openly with Captain Morgan Le Draco spoke to her in an undefinable, but nevertheless profoundly impacting way.

He didn't pry, just smiled, that disarming, devastating twist of his mouth, and her heart, nigh on smitten with him already, flip-flopped. Other parts of her did strange, not altogether unpleasant, things too. Things that had never occurred with any other man

Stop this nonsense at once, Shona. You may be a

bashful misfit, but you're level-headed and prudent.

Tish tosh, her heart scoffed. *Remember your mad dash to the lake? How prudent was that?*

Worry rendered her answering smile somewhat weaker and less remarkable. How would he react to her tainted history?

A fortune hunter wouldn't care.

Enough.

With firm resolve, she banished the cynical, pessimistic voice jeering in her ear to a remote niche in her mind. "I fear my reasons for accompanying the Needhams here aren't altogether pleasant ones."

"I'm sorry to hear that." Though acute interest shone in his eye, he didn't probe for more information.

"It's a long, disagreeable tale," she ventured, not yet certain she wanted to share the ugliness with him.

"I'd be honored to hear it, but please don't feel obligated to tell me." He absently grazed his long fingers over his jaw. "I understand some things are difficult to discuss."

Somehow, she knew he did understand.

What was *his* story? She'd like to hear his too.

And because he had permitted Shona her privacy, her pride and dignity, she wanted to tell him. Wanted him to hear the truth from her before someone whispered an exaggerated or false account and tainted her in his estimation.

"The abbreviated version is that my mother tried to have my half-sister, now the Duchess of Harcourt, murdered for her fortune. I inherited if Alexa died. Mother was sent to an Australian penal colony for the rest of her life. The Needhams graciously took me in for as long as I desired. Mrs. Needham is my half-sister Alexa's maternal aunt."

Because Katrina was their daughter, Shona had hesitatingly agreed to join the Needhams at the house party. Also, Alexa, whom Shona adored, had written to say she planned on attending, and Shona hadn't seen either since Season's end.

Another purpose had motivated her as well.

She'd accepted the Needhams' generosity for nearly two years. Of age, with no marriage prospects and none likely to ever arise, Shona had determined the time had come for her to return to Wedderford

Abbey, take over the running of the estate, and assume her role as Lord of Parliament.

Her heart and stomach quivered.

Those might be considered brave things, mightn't they?

A little raggedy-around-the-edges smile softened the corners of her mouth.

Perhaps wee, verra tiny courageous things.

She couldn't hide from her destiny any longer or continue to take advantage of the Needhams' benevolence. They hadn't been informed of her decision yet, because she wanted to inform Alexa first since her husband, the Duke of Harcourt, was Shona's guardian.

Only for one more day.

The duke had graciously overseen the estate and managed her modest inheritance. Through his financial finesse, he'd parlayed her funds into a credible fortune. More importantly, Wedderford was now solvent, and with continued diligence, the estate might become more so. She'd continue to rely upon his guidance once she took over the management, at least until she retained a trustworthy agent.

The last steward had conspired with Mama, and he too had been sent to the penal colony.

She veered the captivating man beside her a covert glance.

Captain Le Draco looked straight ahead, his brows slightly drawn together, seemingly lost in his own thoughts, and she squelched a wistful sigh.

How she envied Katrina's and Alexa's composure, their confidence and sophistication. And yes, she envied the cousins their handsome, loving husbands. Both their graces openly adored their wives.

Not that she wanted to be a duke's wife.

Her saturated gown didn't cause the shiver padding down her spinal column.

No indeed. Shona didn't even begin to aspire to such heights.

That notion terrified her far worse than being humble Lady Atterberry. Gads, it had taken months to accept the Chancery Court's decision granting her the title. Alexa, as the eldest daughter, should've inherited the title, but the court had bestowed it on Shona instead.

With a small start, she realized the captain had turned his one arresting blue eye on her, his mouth curved into a faint ribbon of a smile.

Shona's stomach tumbled over itself, and she tripped over her own feet.

Och, a newborn lamb is more nimble.

His firm hand at her elbow steadied her as new heat rushed to her cheeks.

What had they been discussing?

Oh, yes. Why she'd come with the Needhams.

"The Needhams are the loveliest people. Their daughter, Katrina, the Duchess of Pendergast, is a dear friend. I don't know what I'd have done without them." And she didn't. As awkward and gauche as she remained, she'd been a veritable social disaster when they'd taken her in. She owed them much.

"I'm truly sorry for your suffering, Shona."

Captain Le Draco had used her given name.

Most impudent of him. Quite beyond the pale.

And she didn't object at all.

"It must've been unbearably difficult for you."

Compassion rendered his voice husky and thick, and for an instant, Shona gaped, owl-like in amazement.

Except for the Needhams, Harcourt, and Alexa, no one had ever expressed any sympathy for her situation. She swallowed against the tangled knot constricting her throat, and blinked away tears she hadn't realized had sprung to her eyes.

She wrapped his coat a bit tighter around her shoulders. "Thank you. It was quite awful at first. But the passage of time has helped. That, and being surrounded by people I know care for me."

Seemingly of its own accord, her finger touched his marred cheek, the merest feathering over the rigid flesh. Brazen, that. And wholly invasive, and inappropriate, particularly since she'd known him all of twenty or thirty brief minutes.

Why did she feel this compelling need to comfort Captain Le Draco? To touch him? Such a powerful, overwhelming need that she kicked aside her usual shyness and reticence?

"What about you, Captain?" Her confidence hadn't yet grown enough to address him by his given name too. "I imagine it's been most difficult for you as well. Does it still hurt?"

She softly pressed her pads against the contorted flesh.

He seized her hand and held it to his ravaged cheek, his eyes closed, eyelashes trembling as if he were in pain or overcome by extreme sentiment.

"Yes."

4

One gruff, heart-wrenching syllable.

Shona wasn't sure which question Captain Le Draco answered. Both, most likely.

So hard for men. They had to suppress their more vulnerable emotions, hide their tender sentiments behind a stalwart disposition and detached facade for fear of appearing weak or unmanly.

"May I ask what happened?"

Once more her gumption flabbergasted her. Nonetheless, she needed to know. Not out of morbid curiosity, or because she was a prying busybody. But because, from the first moment her eyes had collided with his, she'd recognized a fellow damaged spirit. Perhaps, if she knew, she might help him. Reassure him. Bring him some small degree of comfort.

Why she should think an acquaintance of less than an hour had the ability to do any such thing made no sense. Was absolutely out of character, too. And yet, she had to try.

He unhurriedly opened his eyelids, his expression brooding and intense, the angle of his face marble hard.

Ah, here lurked the *Dragon*.

More than a mite unnerving, truth to tell.

To stifle the sudden nervousness bombarding her, she snagged the edge of her lower lip between her teeth. If she hadn't seen the captain's tender, kindhearted side, she would've been blushing and stammering an apology for her boorish inquiry. Or hotfooting it straight to the house, vowing to remain in her locked chamber, buried beneath the bedcoverings until time to depart.

Initially, when she'd realized who he was, she couldn't reconcile the gentle, considerate man who'd risked his life to the legendary soldier's exploits. However, the man before her was every bit the fierce warrior.

A wee shiver scampered down her backbone.

A good man to have on one's side, she'd wager. But most definitely not one she wanted as a foe.

Captain Le Draco's features remained unyielding, a muscle flexing in his jaw, as the silence stretched awkward and uncomfortable between them.

Her heart plunged to her stomach, and she fisted her hand that clutched his coat. So much for tenacity and fortitude. She'd gone too far. Presumed too much. Pushed too hard. "Forgive me, please. I ought not—"

"A fireworks explosion last summer." His carefully flat tone couldn't disguise the trace of pain, piercing and raw, glinting in his bleak eye.

"*Och*— Oh."

She considered his strong features. His disfigurement didn't bother her. Mayhap because she'd never seen him otherwise. Or perhaps, as a consequence of her appearance being judged and often found lacking, outward trappings weren't all that important to her.

"I assumed the injury a military wound," she said.

He shook his head, his tobacco-brown hair dragging across sculpted shoulders she itched to explore. The wry, slightly brittle smile he summoned didn't fool her. For all of Captain Morgan Le Draco's casual indifference, the explosion had damaged his soul every bit as much as his face.

"Nothing so honorable. My regiment was passing a fireworks manufacturer in West London when the blast occurred. Several people died, and many more were seriously injured." Grazing his eyepatch with two square fingertips, he murmured, a near challenge in his suddenly rough voice, "I'm not just blind. I lost the eye entirely."

Poor, poor mon.

Captain Le Draco canted his head, his gaze direct and probing, as if he expected her to recoil in revulsion or abhorrence.

Only fulminating sympathy tunneled through her veins. Which couldn't account for the delicious, comforting sensation burgeoning behind her ribs, near her heart.

"Well, I think you look quite dashing and

altogether very mysterious." With entirely too much unfettered masculine allure. She waggled her eyebrows to ease the sudden tension surrounding them.

He laughed, a joy-filled burble that began quietly but grew in intensity until his broad shoulders and chest shuddered. His mirth gradually dwindled into a lazy chuckle. The raffish smile he gave her spurred a renewed heating of her person, right down to her toes squishing against the crisp grass.

His big palm covered her hand resting on his forearm. "Lady Atterberry, I believe you are quite the most wonderfully, splendidly original woman I've ever met. And you have the most expressive eyes I've ever seen."

He chuckled once more, his deep, rich laugh teasing her ears.

Shona could've lived a year on that sweet praise but wasn't foolish or gullible enough to read more into his words than what was there.

Nevertheless, thrilled she'd lightened his mood, she grinned and bobbed her head in what she hoped was a quaint manner. "Thank you, kind sir."

He chuckled again, and her heart took wing.

When he laughed, his face lit up, and she quite forgot—*wished that he could too*—he was scarred.

Suddenly, the prospect of the week-long house party didn't seem so dreadful. Not if she might spend part of the time in Captain Le Draco's fascinating company.

But did he feel the same?

She slanted him a peek.

A half-smile still bent his molded mouth.

She'd hate to be a nuisance, hanging on his coat sleeves, wondering if kindness prompted his tolerant presence. If he felt… Well, she wasn't sure what she wanted him to feel.

Anything but charity. Or pity. Or ridicule.

Those she couldn't bear, coming from him.

They made the lawns, leaving the grove's cooling shelter behind. Rather than direct her across the verdant expanse, he steered her 'round the perimeter.

From this angle, she could view three sides of the Davenswood.

Under a rainbow of parasols, a few bolder guests

milled the terrace now, and two more laden coaches stood parked before the entry.

No one had spied Shona and the captain yet, but when they did…

She slowed her steps, a fresh wave of angst buffeting her. Engaged in conversation with the captain, she'd failed to consider how she'd enter the manor undetected. Probably impossible given the throng present.

What did it matter?

Even if the Olsons hadn't spread word of her misadventure, by evening's end, every guest would likely know of her ineptness. Well then, what better time to implement her budding fortitude, square her shoulders, lift her chin, and make light of the mishap?

With Captain Le Draco at her side, empowering her, the once momentous feat seemed quite possible.

But first… "Captain Le Draco, I need to retrieve the belongings I left inside the conservatory."

An increasing number of guests now took advantage of the shade at the rear of the manor. Morgan swept his gaze over them before casually angling his body, creating a buffer between Shona and those on the terrace. "I'll gather your things after I've seen you to the house. We'll use the kitchen entrance and the stairway there."

"You know the manor that well?" She sliced him a surprised glance, her pretty eyes wide, the color only slightly lighter than the thick sable lashes framing them.

Did she know her gaze revealed everything she thought? As transparent as water in a glass. That was bloody refreshing.

In answer, he lifted a shoulder. "Allen Wimpleton and I are great friends. I've spent a good deal of time here over the years."

After Mother died, more time than at his own, the next estate over.

Though Wimpleton was in line to inherit a viscountcy, and Morgan's family had clawed and clambered their way into Society's lower levels, the two had become fast friends at Eton.

"What did you leave there?"

"A book, my parasol, a bonnet, and my gloves." Frail color tinted her cheeks.

So adorable how she blushed at the least provocation.

"Lady Addlebertie." Sheltered beneath her garish parasol, Mrs. Olson stood at the veranda's edge, wildly fluttering her lacy handkerchief.

Shona stiffened, and clamped her lower lip between her teeth.

Pulling his mouth into a firm line, Morgan speared the termagant a scathing look.

Addlebertie, indeed. Mean-spirited crone. All because Shona refused her son's mewling attention.

"Ignore her, Shona, and keep moving." He hadn't meant to be so forward, but addressing her by her name came so naturally that he'd blundered again. He took her elbow, and hurrying her along, kept one eye trained on the terrace.

Raising her voice to a near indecorous shout, Mrs. Olson waved even more vigorously. "Yooohooo."

As she'd no doubt intended, numerous guests turned their curious regard toward Morgan and Shona.

Devil fly away with her.

He loathed low-hitting harridans, targeting those they deemed weaker than or inferior to themselves.

"Lady Addle-bertie. Your sister arrived and inquires after you." A triumphant smile wreathing her face, Mrs. Olson cried in a singsong tone, "Oh, and as you requested, a bath has been drawn for you *and* Captain Le Draco."

She made it sound base and dirty. As if something untoward had occurred.

Glancing round to ensure she'd captured her audience's rapt attention, she asked, "Did you enjoy your, ah … *swim* together?"

At her foul inference, Shona released a distressed little gasp.

The sound tore at Morgan's heart.

In that instance, he almost forgot he was a gentleman and told Mrs. Olson precisely where her wayward husband was and whom he was buggering this month.

Instead, Morgan leveled his good eye on her with a glower that had cowed many men.

Shona's hand tightened on his arm. "Captain?"

He glanced downward, somewhat surprised at the brilliant resolve narrowing her eyes. She'd relaxed her grip on his jacket, and the swell of tantalizing, pale honey-toned breasts peeked at him.

With supreme will, he hauled his focus from the delightful view.

She jutted her adorable, determined chin in the veranda's direction. "Let's enter through yonder French window. Shall we?"

Ah, she meant to go on the offense, did she?

Splendid, and sure to be most entertaining. And he'd be right beside her to slay any dragons who dared harass her.

Starting with fire-breathing Mrs. Olson.

"Are you certain?" He knew Mrs. Olson's type. They fought dirty.

"Oh, I'm certain." Shona gave a small, creaky laugh and shoved damp curls off her forehead. "At some point, a person has to make a stand, no matter the consequences."

The slash of her lips and the stubborn set of her shoulders said much. Head high, she glided to the veranda.

The guests, sensing something was about to occur, faced Morgan and Shona as they approached.

Mrs. Olson and a trio of her more vicious cronies, as well as their high-in-the-instep daughters, clustered toward the veranda's front, their heads as close together as their parasols permitted.

No need to speculate what—*who*—they nattered about.

As Shona stepped onto the pavers, they lifted their lofty noses and regarded her coolly, all the while studiously avoiding looking in Morgan's direction.

Cowards.

He arced his mouth into a cynical smile. He ought to be used to it by now.

To Shona's credit, her expression remained impassive, though her hold on his arm was anything but.

He'd sport crescent marks from her nails, for

certain.

Although, unless someone inspected her grip closely, they'd not be able to tell. She'd mastered a blasé countenance well.

Morgan, on the other hand, couldn't resist driving a barb or two home. "Lady Stratham I do hope your *husband* is in attendance with you. I've yet to meet a more accomplished archer."

Morgan couldn't recall if Lord Stratham even delved in archery, but the whole of society knew his wife possessed a voracious appetite for young footmen.

Stable hands. Valets. Drivers.

"And Mrs. Dundercroft?" Morgan grinned when she reluctantly forced herself to meet his gaze, her mouth skewed downward as if she'd eaten a large, wriggling spider. "Did I see in the broad sheets that felicitations are in order? Your son is recently wed, is he not?"

He'd eloped to Gretna Green with an actress of questionable repute last month.

A few amused titters hummed through the crowd.

Not all foe then.

Many of the more considerate guests, after the first few titillating moments, had turned their attentions elsewhere.

Thank God.

Both women's jaws drooped wide as a pelican's before they snapped their mouths shut and pinned him with an irate glare.

Shona's pink lips twitched, but she judiciously brought them under control and boldly met the perusal of each person staring at her.

Some rudely or openly curious. Others compassionate and supportive. And a few, like her tormentors, gloating. She weathered their scrutiny like a champion: countenance regal, gaze inscrutable, the merest sardonic smile bending her mouth.

Something akin to pride welled in Morgan's chest as an unidentified feeling wriggled behind his ribs.

And then, by God, the nameless sentiment had the cheeky tenacity to take root in his chest before settling in like an uninvited guest intending to stay. Indefinitely.

Bugger and blast!

He couldn't permit himself to feel anything for Shona.

Nonetheless, he could protect her, champion her this week. Give her confidence in herself so that when a worthy man came along, she'd not feel undeserving or afraid.

Hand still cupping her elbow, he steered her past the neck-craning onlookers. He'd nearly made the first set of French doors when Francine, the eldest, freckle-faced, turnip-shaped Dundercroft sister unfurled her fan, casting her cohorts a smirking smile.

"Lady Atterberry, I can only presume you weren't aware—being a Scot and all—but *ladies* don't swim in lakes. And most especially not attired in walking gowns."

So, the older harpies had delegated the task of hassling and besmirching Shona to the younger nincompoops. Indeed, rotten fruit didn't fall far from the tree, but unfortunately, everyone was subjected to the decaying stench when they came near.

Shona blanched then, husbanding strength Morgan

couldn't help but respect, she calmly raked her benign gaze over her tormenter.

Miss Dundercroft's smile slipped.

"I didn't go swimming. I stumbled and fell into the lake. I most certainly would've drowned had Captain Le Draco not risked his life to rescue me." She veered a glance, the merest bit accusatory, toward Mrs. Olson. "Unlike others who stood by the whole while as the captain labored to bring us both to shore."

"I cannot swim," Mrs. Olson mumbled, suddenly absorbed in her parasol's unremarkable handle.

Your son can.

"I'll just bet the captain struggled. Mightily, no doubt." The younger Dundercroft chit, Miss Lyselle, snickered. She bobbed her head, exchanging a secretive look with her sister.

Where Shona's figure was deliciously curved, the flesh firm and creamy, the thick-set Dundercrofts' forms were… Well, weren't. And they had the ill-fated tendency to become mottled with unflattering reddish blotches whenever they were excited.

Like now.

"Such *gaucherie*," Miss Lyselle cooed, batting her stubby lashes. "But to parade about in a wet gown. Surely you realize how scandalous that is?"

No worse than a number of *tonnish* women who deliberately dampened their gowns, some abstaining from wearing undergarments beneath the sheer fabric.

For instance, as Miss Penelope Rossington, now standing between the Dundercroft disasters, was wont to do.

"And precisely how was Lady Atterberry to avoid doing so when her dry clothing is inside the manor?" Morgan's question had the younger Dundercroft chit blinking her eyes in confusion.

Aware of the rapt gazes affixed on the exchange, Morgan glanced at Miss Rossington. The petite beauty possessed the morals of a Covent Garden prostitute. Before his accident, she'd offered herself to him more than once. Practically begged him to take her, as he recalled.

Now she could scarcely bear to look at him.

Definitely one of the most superficial, self-serving damsels to wriggle her way into the *haut ton's* favor in a goodly while.

The worst hellcat of the group, she sidled forward, and his gut clenched, his blood burning in his veins. Miss Rossington's penchant for jealousy and cruelty knew no bounds. She'd sink her verbal claws into Shona, leaving deep, bleeding grooves, then laugh at the pain and lasting scars she'd caused.

Yet, Shona needed to face her nemeses. Needed to stand up to these she-devils. For her sake, she must learn to.

He might've known her for a very short time, but he possessed an uncanny ability to read people. Beneath her reticent exterior, probably the result of ongoing abuse and bullying, a vivacious spirit simmered.

Why he'd decided he was the person to help her blossom, he couldn't fathom.

It just felt right.

Miss Rossington spared him the briefest, most cursory of glances, her lips curling slightly as she shuddered when her regard lit upon his ravaged face.

"Come along, Lady Atterberry," he urged, almost

sighing in relief when Lady Wimpleton, accompanied by two attractive women, stepped through the French window onto the flagstones. He'd bet his other eye that one of them was Shona's sister.

"However do you expect to find yourself a husband when you behave like a hoyden?" Miss Rossington asked, while haughtily taking Shona's measure. She wrinkled her nub of a nose as if she smelled offal.

Shona barely spared her a glance.

That's it. Don't take the bait.

"A dowdy Scottish dumpling. Clumsy too. Falling into the lake. Chuffy thighs and all. What a sight that must've been." Miss Rossington laughed nastily, and a few of the others joined her unkind cackling.

However, several other guests conferred disapproving glances upon her, including Manchester, the formidable Marquis of Sterling, and the two elegant ladies with Lady Wimpleton. Neither of which shied away from Morgan's face either.

He liked them already.

More so that they looked ready to filet the vermin

targeting Shona.

They gracefully wended their way through the crowd, smooth brows furrowed, their focus fixed on her.

"It's a good thing you've plenty of money." Envy, jeering and shrill, tinged Miss Rossington's venomous words. "You'll require an enormous sum to land a husband. Else you'd remain an unmarried tabby."

"Miss Rossington." Sterling leveled her a baleful look as he picked a piece of lint from his immaculate, disgustingly expensive, first-stare-of-fashion coat. "Perhaps you ought to consider the dozen or so much more important characteristics which would cause gentlemen to shun a—" he cocked a skeptical brow while raking her from toe to top with a critical eye, "*lady*."

Touché, Sterling.

With that barbed comment, just this side of an insult, he sauntered away.

Hands balled, Miss Rossington glared at his retreating figure, the merest hint of longing shadowing her face.

Outwardly composed, Shona sent Sterling's back a small, grateful smile as she drew to a stop beside Miss Rossington.

Morgan lightly squeezed her trembling arm.

He had no compunction about telling Miss Rossington to go to hell and shag the devil, but he didn't want to shock or upset Shona.

Even with her damp ringlets tumbling down her back and his too-large coat draped around her shoulders, she possessed a regal presence. A gentle and sweet essence that far surpassed Miss Rossington's—or any of the other ladies', truth to tell—superficial splendor.

Shona's beauty emanated from within, and when combined with her comely face and perfect form, she was an absolute incomparable.

Why couldn't everyone else see it?

Sterling recognizes her exceptionality.

Were they blind?

At the absurdity, he checked a caustic laugh.

Hell, he *was* blind in one eye, and from the instant he'd seen her off-balance and tottering, about to plunk into the lake, he'd recognized her uniqueness. It had called to him, enticing and irresistible, across the expanse.

Such pure, unsullied loveliness was most rare.

Perhaps some of the others did sense it, and that was why they attacked her.

A swift survey of those assembled revealed multiple gentlemen's more than casual interest. The realization slammed into Morgan with the force of a battering ram. He wanted to plant them all facers. Tell them to direct their damned regard elsewhere.

But he hadn't the right. Never would have.

If Shona ever became aware of her allure, bloomed into the rare and extraordinary flower he'd glimpsed, she'd have men groveling at her feet.

"Did you have something you wanted to say, Lady Atterberry?" Her rouged mouth arching upward, Miss Rossington slanted her head and blinked innocently. "Perhaps you want to ask me for advice?" She leaned nearer Shona, and sotto voce said, "On how you might become more attractive to gentlemen?"

5

A *part from exposing nearly all of my bosoms, as you do?*

If Miss Rossington sneezed, Shona expected her generous bounty to leap free of the dangerously low, lace-edged bodice. Might blacken both her eyes in the process.

She scarcely knew the woman, had never done anything to deserve her contempt and vindictiveness. An hour ago, cheeks burning, she'd have ducked her head and fled, mortified to her toes, into the house to hide in her chamber for at least a day. Likely the remainder of the week.

Now however…

Brow arched, she refused to quell under Miss

Rossington's spite.

She would rather have gnawed on a hog farmer's manure-coated boots than let Captain Le Draco see her browbeaten and intimidated.

He was strong and courageous—and she wanted to be too.

For him.

Which made no sense whatsoever, but she refused to analyze her feelings further.

He had her at sixes and sevens, but perhaps that was what she needed. Something—*someone*—whose esteem motivated her to become what she'd only dared dream she might ever be.

Besides, it was far past time she spoke her mind. Her self-respect demanded it.

How could she possibly oversee her estate or fulfill the role of Lord of Parliament if she remained a timid, self-effacing nit?

Shaking her head, she marshaled a closed-mouth smile, despite quaking inside like a leaf pummeled by a furious gale. "No, Miss Rossington. I can't conceive why I'd ever need *your* advice."

The malevolent chit bestowed such a condescending look upon Shona, she almost recoiled.

"Oh, I'll wager you do, my dearest, *dearest* dowd," Miss Rossington simpered. "More than you can possibly realize. Instruction on that and perhaps on how to persuade a man to kiss you." She sighed dramatically and shook her perfectly coiffed blonde head. "I'm not altogether positive the latter is feasible, however."

This entire conversation was so ridiculous, so beyond the pale, that Shona marveled at the woman's perseverance. Why was she so determined to humiliate her? Miss Rossington's behavior bordered on irrational.

Even Lord Sterling's set down hadn't deterred her.

A wise woman would've ignored Miss Rossington. Dismissed her behavior for what it was. Unprovoked, immature, undeserved—*unhinged?*—jealousy and contempt.

A surge of rebelliousness seized Shona, and she jutted her chin upward.

Enough of turning the other cheek. Cowering in

diffidence. Feeling inferior and unworthy.

"I'll accept that wager, Miss Rossington."

Miss Rossington's peridot eyes grew round, her artificial smile faltering. She licked her lips, her harried gaze darting here and there. "Pardon?"

A few onlookers' mouths glided upward at her discomfiture.

Was she nervous she'd been caught in her own snare?

As well she should be.

"I said, I accept your challenge." Enjoying the moment, Shona stepped away from the captain. Resting her hand on Miss Rossington's trembling shoulder, she placed her mouth directly beside Miss Rossington ear and whispered for her alone, "Before the week's end, I'll have been kissed by the most attractive man here."

Perhaps, if God were kind, more than kissed.

How Shona meant to accomplish the task, she hadn't yet conceived. She'd recruit Katrina and Alexa to help with her appearance, mayhap even dare such artifice as cosmetics. If that was what it took to accomplish the task.

But the kissing bit?

Well, that Shona would have to maneuver on her own. With the only man present she had any desire to kiss.

She stalwartly refrained from so much as peeking in Captain Le Draco's direction.

Hopefully, he'd oblige and wouldn't be too put off at her using him to win the wager. But how was she to prove he'd kissed her? She wasn't about to procure witnesses, for pity's sake.

Well, she'd worry about that particular later. She had a whole week to work that detail out.

Miss Rossington, her expression pinched and most enjoyably nonplussed, opened her mouth.

"I think you've said quite enough. I'll tolerate no more," Captain Le Draco said, his tone and formidable countenance brooking no argument.

The Dragon had decided to put in an appearance.

With an irritated huff, Miss Rossington spun around, and after seizing the elder Dundercroft sister's arm, propelled the befuddled chit to the entrance.

Shona slid him a contemplative glance.

Mouth slightly hitched, his arms folded across his impossibly broad chest, he regarded her with a bemused expression.

He couldn't possibly have heard her whispered words, yet from the amusement in his glittering, heavy-lidded gaze, she'd be bound he had a very good notion of what she'd just vowed.

He didn't appear the least averse either.

"Shona?"

Shona whirled around.

Alexa and Katrina, along with Lady Wimpleton, stood behind her.

Oh, splendid.

A perfectly timed arrival.

Still attired in their traveling costumes, Alexa's a brilliant violet and Katrina's a deep rose, both were inarguably exquisite, the epitome of *haut ton* elegance.

And she adored them.

Shona's confidence soared at the deferential glances now sidling her way. A wonder what influential company accomplished. After exchanging exuberant embraces with her sister and friend, she motioned down her soggy front and offered a lop-sided grin. "I had a slight mishap."

"So we heard and can quite clearly see, dear one," Alexa said, a glint of disquiet in her gaze. "You're quite all right, though?"

Shona nodded. "Yes." She searched past them. "Where are their graces?"

Katrina chuckled and flicked an errant strand of hair off her cheek. "Enjoying a dram with our host."

"You gave us quite a fright. We'd only just arrived and heard you'd fallen into the lake." Alexa snagged Shona's elbow, hugging it to her side. "Come, let's get you upstairs." She graciously left off the "and cleaned up" part.

"Your bath is ready," Lady Wimpleton said, smiling first at Shona then Captain Le Draco. "Yours too, Captain. But you'd better hurry before it grows cold."

"Many thanks, my lady." Captain Le Draco angled his head differentially.

Katrina wrapped an arm around Shona's waist in

what could only be considered a protective gesture. "Dinner's in less than two hours, and I haven't yet washed the travel dust off."

Before they could trot her inside, Shona stalled them. She waved at the captain silently observing the reunion. "Please, permit me to introduce you to the brave man who very well may have saved my life at no little peril to his own."

Kind-hearted and compassionate, Alexa and Katrina immediately faced the captain, pleasant, expectant smiles framing their mouths. Shona needn't have worried they'd balk at his appearance. Expressions open and accepting, neither as much as blinked, nor did they stare at the glaring mark slashing his cheek.

His mouth edged upward the tiniest bit, and joy billowed in Shona's silly heart, like a sail on a windy day. Such a simple, wee thing, but it obviously meant much to him.

Had he experienced a great deal of rejection because of his face?

Probably.

Such shallowness appalled and angered her. She could've hugged Alexa and Katrina until they squealed.

"Captain Le Draco, my sister, Her Grace, Alexandra, the Duchess of Harcourt, and my dearest friend, Her Grace, Katrina, the Duchess of Pendergast. Alexa, Katrina, may I present Captain Morgan Le Draco?"

Captain Le Draco made a neat leg, his bow graceful and gallant, despite his unkempt appearance and large frame. His mane of almost-dry chestnut hair spilled forward at the motion. "I am deeply honored, Your Graces."

"And we are forever in your debt, Captain. Shona is most precious to us," Alexa said, her eyes tear-brightened. "Now, if you'll please excuse us. I'm sure you understand she must set her appearance to right." Her warm smile said much. "Thank you again."

"Indeed, Captain. Please, won't you join us in the floral garden room before dinner so that we might become better acquainted? I should like to introduce you to my husband." Katrina's invitation rang with sincerity. "You remind me of him. He was a privateer before he inherited the dukedom."

Giving Captain Le Draco a mischievous look, Shona chuckled. "He was known as The Saint of the Sea."

An answering grin lit the captain's face and eye. "I shall look forward to it, Your Grace."

Whether he wanted it or not, unfailingly loyal, the Harcourts and Pendergasts had taken the captain under their wings. He'd helped one of their own and was welcome in their circle henceforth. For certain, he didn't seem a man who needed others' approval. Still, Shona couldn't help but believe he appreciated it, nonetheless.

"There you are, Morgan." An older, stern-faced man, greatly resembling the captain, marched across the terrace, his walking stick angrily rapping the flagstones with each pronounced step. He spared the women the briefest of glances—Shona the most fleeting. "You left before I had a chance to tell you. I've made arrangements for you to sail to Barbados in a fortnight."

A horse's kick to Morgan's gut would've hurt less than the shocked dismay darkening Shona's velvety eyes. Her effervescent smile faded, and the slash of her lips as she averted her gaze screeched, "Duplicitous knave."

How could she feel betrayed or deceived?

They'd only just met.

A relationship couldn't be forged or sentiments engaged in an hour, no matter how enjoyable the time spent or entrancing the company.

Stupid fool. You don't think she feels the same irresistible draw you do?

Just as well his father had ruined things then.

She couldn't harbor any false notions about Morgan.

A future together was impossible.

After this house party ended, he didn't even know where his next meal would come from. Or where he'd live, for that matter.

His landlord had raised his rent, and Morgan hadn't the blunt to pay it. He'd been borrowing from Viola, keeping immaculate records so that one day he could repay her.

At present, his options were limited, and growing more so. Sign on as a deckhand. Or perhaps find a position as a miner or laborer. Maybe even a saloon strongman. The latter appealed in a perverse sort of way. It was a profession where people either weren't subjected to his face or didn't mind the contorted flesh.

As Shona was bustled away, Morgan bit his tongue to restrain the foul oath hammering at the back of his teeth and that he ached to hurl at his father's head. He'd not have her thinking him an uncivilized beast. His appearance was monstrous enough. She needn't witness loutish, uncouth behavior as well.

Look back. Just one glance.

He gave a disgusted snort, raking his fingers through his tousled hair.

Oh, for God's sake, man. Make up your bloody mind.

Father scowled, and, just to aggravate him further,

Morgan shook his head, sending his hair billowing about his shoulders.

Father's inscrutable gaze tightened, but he remained silent.

For a damned, blessed change.

Just before she stepped across the threshold, Shona cast a sorrowful, confused gaze over her shoulder, her tiny smile fragile and bittersweet.

Morgan wanted to let loose with a litany of curses at the pain shadowing her pansy-like eyes, and kick his heels up that she'd wanted one more glimpse.

Once she'd disappeared indoors, he cut his gaze to his father and jerked his chin, indicating his sire should follow him. He didn't trust himself to speak at present, and what he had to say wasn't meant for delicate ears or polite company.

Not that he gave a parson's blessing what most of these people thought of him.

If Allen Wimpleton hadn't stooped to cajoling, Morgan wouldn't have even been here. And if he'd known his father intended to trundle over from Milwick Park, the neighboring estate, he'd have stayed in London regardless.

Besides, damn him for a fool, Morgan knew Wimpleton's insistence he attend the party was motivated by pity as much as friendship. He'd offered, several times in fact, to extend Morgan funds, which he'd firmly refused.

Accepting food and lodgings from friends chafed his arse raw. But money?

No. He'd too much pride.

He'd refused Viola too, until she'd burst into tears, accusing him of being a heartless beast. That she couldn't sleep at night for worry about him. She'd looked at him with those great hazel-blue, tear-filled eyes, and he'd yielded. Mother had left her a modest sum, and it was those funds she sacrificed for Morgan.

He rubbed his brow above his missing eye, still fuming at his father's unmitigated and unrepentant gall. Morgan's gaze lit on the conservatory. Perfect. He needed to fetch Shona's things anyway.

He crinkled his brow. When was the last time he'd been inside the greenhouse? At least a decade ago. Yes, that tryst with—

Never mind.

He stalked down the serpentine gravel pathway, not caring a whit if his father followed or kept up.

Devil fly away with him. He'd gone too bloody far this time.

Morgan meant to put him in his place, leave no doubt as to where he stood. Let his father disown him as he'd threatened for years. It would be a relief, truth to tell.

Reaching the hothouse, Morgan swiftly scanned the interior. Empty and silent except for the fountain's babbling. A mourning dove, head cocked and curiously peeking in the other doors, took flight as he stalked inside. Several feminine fallalls lay upon a quaint scrolled bench. Giving his ire a few moments to calm, he gathered the accoutrements before facing his father.

"What has you in such a foul mood?" Father fished his perfectly starched and folded handkerchief from his pocket and mopped his ruddy face. "Or perhaps I should say, fouler than usual mood?"

Only foul around you.

"Father, I've made it abundantly clear that I shall

never, and I do mean never, take any part of your enterprises. It sickens me to think of exploiting overworked and abused slaves for gain. You know I'm an abolitionist and abhor everything about slavery."

He draped Shona's gloves over his forearm before hooking the parasol handle on his wrist. A whiff of her perfume wafted upward. He'd never met a woman who smelled so enticing. He wanted to bury his face in her neck, between her bountiful, marvelous breasts, and inhale her intoxicating scent.

If wishes were horses…

"I've given you a year to come to your senses," his father retorted, wrath sparking in his azure eyes.

Morgan's eyes. Except his lacked the mercenary, cold-hearted, self-serving, calculating glint.

"I would've stayed in the cavalry, but you stripped me of that choice."

Father had tried to force Morgan's hand. Had thought by resigning his commission, he'd manipulate Morgan to do his bidding.

"Lost that gamble, you miserable baggage," Morgan muttered, the sting of betrayal still strong.

"Wots that? Stop your mumbling and speak up." His father cupped his ear. "You know my hearing's not what it once was."

"I'm not going to Barbados. Put it out of your head."

"Pray tell me then, what other prospects have you?"

Lovely to know one's parent held one in such high regard.

Father squinted at the items Morgan held, his mouth hardening into a grim line. "You're grossly disfigured."

Thank you for reminding me in such a considerate manner.

"You barely have two coins to rub together."

Actually, I have three.

"And I know full well Viola's buying your clothes and lending you funds to pay for your rooms."

Sad, but true.

"Have you no pride?"

No. Not a whole lot anymore.

"Taking advantage of your sister's benevolent

nature?"

She's truly angelic. Almost as sweet as Shona.

"I'll find employment." Morgan glimpsed the book's gold-lettered, leather spine before tucking the volume under his arm. *The Works of Robert Burns.*

The little romantic.

"Just who do you think will employ a man with your—?" Father flapped his hand toward Morgan's face? "Your visage will chase customers away."

"I said I'd find something." Morgan had looked for a clerical or steward position for months. More than one friend had offered him a post, each of which, he'd vow, was hastily created so that Morgan might be presented the situation. He'd declined each, after expressing his gratitude for their thoughtfulness.

Their pity would suffocate him, eventually turn him into a shadow who didn't care whether he lived or died. Not too far from that already, if he were totally honest with himself.

He swept his hair off one shoulder.

Well, he'd just have to seek less refined employment. That was all.

"You're an even bigger fool than I supposed, Morgan," Father jeered. He shook his head and jammed his thumb over his shoulder. "I saw the way you ogled that buxom chit. She has nice tits, I'll give her that. But do you honestly think she'd have *you*?"

Dragging in an exaggerated breath, Morgan closed his eyes and forced himself to count to ten very—*very*—slowly. Sons didn't go around clobbering their offensive fathers. As much as he longed to wipe the smirk off his sire's face, he wouldn't, for Viola's sake.

But by thunder, if Father besmirched or disrespected Shona one more time, Morgan would endure his sister's tears and censure.

He slung his father a reproachful glance. "Since I just met Lady Atterberry and haven't entertained any intention of asking her to be my wife, your point is moot, isn't it?"

Nevertheless, Morgan most definitely had entertained other, less momentous intentions.

His father threw his hands up, his disgust tangible. His utter confusion equally so. "You'd really prefer that I disown you? You'll not get a penny from me.

Milwick will be lost to you. Viola will receive everything."

How often had Morgan heard these same threats?

"She's welcome to all of it. But even she wants no part of your dealings in the tropics. She told me so herself." Morgan cocked his head, trying to understand this man whose seed had created him, but whose character and values were so vastly different. "You have more money than you can spend in a lifetime. Why must you continue with the plantations?"

"Your ignorance is beyond bloody maddening." Aversion warred with contempt in Father's voice, his angular face contorting into one of his lofty sneers. "One can never have enough money. And why do you keep sniveling about the darkies? You can't possibly believe they're our equals. I cannot begin to comprehend your thinking. I truly cannot."

"I'm not the least surprised." Utterly inconceivable that such a deplorable had spawned Morgan. They were as unalike as black was to white. Night was to day.

He looped Shona's bonnet's ribbons around his

fingertips.

Would her skin feel as satiny?

He'd never know.

Hell's bells. Why, even in the midst of a heated argument, did she intrude upon his thoughts?

"So be it." His father considered him for an extended moment, a hint of authentic regret shadowing his eyes. In a blink, the sentiment was gone, replaced by his usual wintery visage. "I'll be for home then. I cannot stay here and remain civil to you." He swiveled toward the door, then swung back, his expression contemplative.

"That Atterberry gel. She's an heiress, ain't she?" Father squinted and nodded slowly, a wily smile pulling his mouth sideways. "Ah, I'm on to your game now, son. You're after her money. Brilliant, I must concede. What do you intend? To seduce the wench?"

6

Two mornings later, Shona tilted her parasol to block the sun as well as the curious glances of the other guests taking strolls about the lawn and gardens. She and Morgan—she'd taken to calling him by his given name when in private—had garnered more than a few whispers and speculative looks since her dunk in the lake.

Let them chatter. She didn't give a fig what any of them thought.

He'd been most attentive since the ill-fated, yet fortunate incident. Not only did he claim her for a walk each morning, Morgan remained at her side during the indoor entertainment too. And as he'd promised, he practiced the waltz with her.

To avoid gossip, they'd agreed to meet prior to breakfast, before the rest of the house roused.

He hadn't exaggerated when he said he was a fair partner. More than fair. So adept, in fact, she felt certain she could maneuver the steps at the masque ball now. It was quite thrilling to be held in such a man's arms. Addictive even.

She left her bed early each morning, to fuss over her attire and toilette in a manner previously alien to her. Thank goodness, she hadn't had to share her chamber after all. She'd not want to have to explain her sudden frenzied interest in her appearance.

She cut him a swift glance, admiring his chiseled profile. She'd miss him.

They'd fallen into a comfortable camaraderie—that was all it could be, of course—and his presence had made the house party the most pleasant she'd ever attended.

Much to her surprise, Lord Sterling had sought her company on several occasions, though she suspected his kindness was due more to his close association with Harcourt than any genuine fascination with her.

It wouldn't be the first time Alexa or Katrina had imposed upon their husbands to encourage their male friends to pay Shona some small attention to lessen her obvious social failings. Shortcomings which seemed so much less noticeable or important when with Morgan.

Whether due to Morgan's stern visage or the presence of her influential relatives, the other guests' treatment of her had improved dramatically. Of course, her self-appointed guardian was rather a fire-breathing dragon to anyone who as much as glanced at her askance. One scorching glare usually sufficed to divert their attention or send them skulking away.

And Shona didn't mind in the least.

For certain, she didn't *need* a male's protection, but she wouldn't deny enjoying the privilege.

"Lady Wimpleton has planned a play for this evening." Shona arched a sardonic eyebrow. "A Greek comedy, no less."

Morgan chuckled, the sound robust with humor and disbelief. "I might find myself otherwise engaged. As might most of the remaining gentlemen she hasn't pressed into assisting her."

"I wish I might join you. But Katrina promised Olivia Wimpleton she'd take part, and so I pledged to attend the performance and support her."

Shona had politely, but firmly, declined to participate. She wasn't about to toddle around wearing a scanty linen garment and a grapevine wreath atop her head. Plus, she hadn't wanted to commit the time to the silly theatrical performance when she'd much prefer to spend it with Morgan.

Mere days ago, the week had seemed interminable, but now it passed much too swiftly for her liking. She found herself regretting that they'd part company in a few short days and she'd be off to her new life as Wedderford's mistress.

Except for Alexa and Katrina splurging and presenting her with a new gown for the masque ball, her birthday yesterday had passed with minimal fanfare, thank goodness. Last night, Shona and Morgan had escaped the charades and card games and spent a wonderful hour sitting beside the lake chatting.

That had been the best part of her one-and-twentieth birthday.

He'd presented her with a handpicked bouquet—she'd lay odds a few of Lady Wimpleton's hothouse blooms were amongst the blossoms—and a beautiful bird he'd whittled.

Never had a gift meant more, and she'd fought sentimental tears as she brushed her fingertips across the nubby wood. That humble carving made with his two hands became her most cherished possession in an instant, worth far more than the considerable jewels included in Wedderford's entailment.

Accepting the token breached social boundaries, but a team of Craiglocky Keep's renowned draft horses couldn't have pried the trinket from her fingers.

The more time she spent with Morgan, the more he captivated her. While others turned their attention aside or avoided him because of his scarred face, she found herself drawn to him more and more.

In truth, she hardly noticed the marks anymore.

"Ho, there." A trio of brown-and-white spaniel pups loped across the lawn, chased by two flustered stable lads.

"The little beasts have escaped again." Morgan

whistled, and the pups changed directions, charging straight toward him and Shona.

She squatted, bracing herself for the onslaught of happy dogs. After their frenzied greeting, including much whining, tail-wagging, and a few slobbery doggy kisses, she stood once more and brushed at her jonquil skirt.

Grass and dirt smudges peppered the area where the pups had tried to clamber into her lap.

"I really do think I may ask the Wimpletons if I might have the smallest one." Grinning, she pointed to a sweet-faced female trying to chew the servant's lapel. "She has a slight limp, and I've always wanted a dog."

"I'm sorry, m'lady, sir." One of the young men bobbed his head in apology. "These be quick ones, and smart too. They've learned how to nose their enclosure open."

"It's quite all right. I adore dogs," Shona said.

A pup might be just the thing to help alleviate the loneliness no doubt awaiting her at Wedderford Abbey. As the young men struggled with the wriggling armfuls, Shona giggled.

Yes, when she left Davenswood Court, she'd have a canine companion with her. She wished she might have more...

She turned to Morgan, and her breath stalled at the rapt expression on his face as he regarded her. Almost as if he were as entranced with her as she feared she was fast becoming with him.

Could it be true?

She'd truly earned the admiration of a man such as he?

A pleasant warmth blossomed through her, starting at her toes and ending with twin pools of heat settling in her cheeks.

Logical miss that she was, she knew better than to make more of the situation than it was. Nevertheless, for the present, she'd cherish this unexpected wonderfulness, and if it meant winning her rash bet against Miss Rossington in the process, so much the better.

Morgan curled his mouth into a smile, partly sensual and partly appreciative, before looping her arm through his elbow, then brazenly laying his hand atop hers. Every now and again, he skimmed his fingers across the back of her hand and electric sparks shot up her arm.

They strolled along in companionable silence.

She hadn't a notion what his thoughts might be and didn't dare indulge in hoping hers might ever come true. But for these few days, she'd enjoy the company of this splendid man and be thankful she'd met him. He'd given her a taste of something she'd never thought to experience.

No one had come right out and said it, but though her family was grateful he'd saved her life and was perfectly lovely to him, more than one had dropped hints that any notion of something more developing between her and Morgan was pure fancy. Almost as if they knew something she didn't, but weren't about to share the unpleasant knowledge with her.

Och. Enough darkling musings. Why waste time with what-ifs and unknowns?

"What are your plans after this week, Morgan?"

Are ye aff yer heid, Shona?

One dark brow shot skyward.

He mightn't have said it, but the implication was clear.

None of your business.

She'd no right to pry, so instead, to disguise her discomfiture, she blurted the first thing that popped to mind. "I'm returning to my familial home in Scotland. I've been away too long as it is, and now that I'm of age, I cannot delay the inevitable."

A distant look shadowed his eyes, and she didn't miss the fact he'd not answered her question.

"You have much on your young shoulders, Shona."

"Not everyone gets to choose their lot in life, and despite the trials I've had, I've been blessed." No one need tell her that her smile held a hint of fragility. "Perhaps, Morgan, you might visit me at Wedderford someday?"

Subtle as a pig in a poke bonnet, that.

It seemed the cheeky boldness that had been dormant for so long had escaped its fetters, much like the rambunctious pups, and she was hard put to control the high-spirited thing.

Morgan pulled her a jot closer to his side, yet sadness tempered his tender smile. "I should very much like to, but I regret I cannot make any such promise, Shona."

Soundly rejected.

"I understand." Humiliation burned her face, and she couldn't flee to her chamber swiftly enough. "Please excuse me—"

"I don't think you do understand." Morgan clasped her hand, gently but firmly, preventing her escape. "I don't make promises I'm not positive I can fulfill. But I do vow every minute I've enjoyed with you these past days has been a privilege. I would be honored if you'd continue to spend time with me."

How could she say no and deny herself a few more precious memories?

How could she say yes and risk losing her heart completely?

Too late.

He raised her hand and brushed his lips across the knuckles. "Please, Shona, say you will."

"Aye." She'd embrace what Fate offered. When she left Davenswood Court, it would be without her heart.

7

Shona smoothed her hands down the front of her gown—a champagne gauze trimmed in lavender, made for Katrina's wedding and not worn since. Eager to look her finest tonight, Shona had asked Alexa's abigail to dress her hair. Toward that end, she'd even donned new stays containing a flattering busk, and at Katrina's encouragement, permitted the slightest application of cosmetics.

They'd fussed over Shona, helping her choose the perfect jewels to complement her attire. And when her toilette was complete, they'd clapped in delight, their faces wreathed in smiles.

She felt quite the loveliest she ever had.

However, she hadn't been able to summon the

nerve to ask them how she might go about enticing a gentleman to kiss her, and she hadn't many days left to win her wager.

Surely such things came naturally if the couple were mutually attracted to each other.

For the fourth time, Shona checked to make sure the amethyst earrings still dangled from her ears and the necklace resting just above her breasts remained centered. She patted the elegant Grecian knot at her nape before brushing her fingers over the parure's matching combs, which swept her hair up on the sides, except for a fringe of soft curls framing her face.

Those new additions were the result of the abigail's considerable skill with scissors and a hot iron.

Fingering one of the playful curls, Shona conceded that the new hair arrangement quite became her. She was womanly enough to admit she wanted to impress Morgan, else why bother with all the falderal?

Whilst getting dressed this evening, she'd made a meaningful decision.

These were the last days before she stepped into her new roles and assumed the responsibilities that went with them. No man had ever stirred her the way Morgan did. She mightn't—probably wouldn't ever have an occasion to—enjoy the attention of such a man again.

So, she intended to seize this chance, come what may. And by Jove, she still planned to seek an opportunity to kiss him. As much to prove Penelope Rossington wrong as to prove to herself that she could.

Though short of tackling the captain and holding him down for a peck on the mouth—fine, something considerably more than a prim peck—she hadn't a clue how she'd accomplish the task.

Nae, not a task.

That sounded far too chore-like, and she didn't believe for a second that kissing Morgan would be anything akin to mucking stalls, polishing the silver, or scouring chamber pots.

Indeed, she imagined the experience would be something much more ethereal and magical. And deliciously carnal too.

Lord, listen to her wanton thoughts. A flush sluiced through her, a wave of chagrined pleasure originating somewhere in her middle and billowing upward to her artfully arranged hair.

Who'd have believed she'd be so easily influenced into risqué behavior?

Certainly not she.

Not before she'd met Captain Morgan-oh-so-wonderfully-fascinating-Le Draco.

What happened to the modest, reserved woman who'd absconded to the hothouse her first day here? If Shona hadn't known better, she'd have believed she'd knocked her noggin when she plunged into the lake, so altered was she.

As she approached the drawing room where she'd agreed to meet the others before dinner, laughter and chatter carried into the corridor. The floral salon farther down the passageway also rang with amusement and animated conversation. Her stomach constricted in apprehension.

You can do this. Remember what you decided. To make these remaining days the most pleasant, the most memorable of your life.

Well, at least the most pleasurably unforgettable

so far. Some of her darker memories she'd never be able to completely dispel.

Dredging up a cordial smile, she entered the drawing room, and standing at the threshold, searched for anyone she might know.

Alexa and Katrina hadn't come down yet. Likely because they'd assisted Shona.

Clutching her fan to still her frolicking nerves, she searched the room again.

Where was Morgan?

Maybe he'd gone to the salon instead.

Harcourt and Pendergast were present, though. Each with a glass in hand, they chatted with several gentlemen, including Mr. Olson. He kept veering her reproachful glances, his chin elevated and expression offended.

What a perfectly horrid misalliance that would've been.

Rather than regard her dip in the lake as calamitous, she thought it rather fortunate now. It spared her further pursuit by that presumptuous, feckless toad. Besides, her rescuer had turned out to be a most fascinating man.

Unfurling her fan, she sought other familiar faces.

Lord Sterling angled his auburn head in greeting, a smile playing round the edges of his mouth as he listened to something elderly Miss Sweeting said.

Shona returned his smile.

Though taciturn and aloof, when she'd encountered him in London, he'd always been unfailingly kind to her, treating her much the way a person would a stray, frightened mongrel.

She continued her search of the crowded room.

Engaged in lively conversation, neither Mr. nor Mrs. Needham had noticed her arrival.

Nodding at something an imposing dame said, Lady Wimpleton offered a welcoming smile from across the room.

What to do?

Stay here or prowl the salon in search of Morgan?

It couldn't hurt to take a peek there.

Waving her fan, more for something to do rather than loiter self-consciously in the entrance, she'd swiveled to leave when a movement caught her attention.

A tall form separated from the shadows in the room's far corner.

Her lungs emptied on a happy sigh.

Morgan.

He drained his tumbler, then set it on a nearby table. Mouth sweeping into a closed-lipped smile, he gave her a devilish wink, seemingly as delighted to see her as she was to see him.

Goodness. She pressed a hand to her cavorting stomach.

What that man did to her with one roguish blink of his eye. Her heart, the ridiculous, flighty thing, flopped about like a brown trout on a river bank.

And her breathing?

Why, it became all breathy and gaspy, too.

Was gaspy a word?

It certainly was a feeling.

Did his heart and lungs do weird things when he saw her as well?

What a lovely, farfetched notion.

Given his declaration this morning, mayhap not as

farfetched as she'd once believed.

From across the distance, his hot, enticing gaze devoured her.

Her thrumming body answered the call with an abandon she hadn't known she possessed.

Wending his way to her side, his focus never strayed as he agilely maneuvered around the guests.

"Lady Atterberry. You look utterly entrancing this evening. A vision for this beleaguered one-eyed soldier to behold." Wearing unadorned black evening togs, his hair pulled into a queue and tied with a narrow black satin ribbon, he emanated pure, virile power.

A pleased blush stole up her cheeks, as he eyed her approvingly, a rakish gleam in his vivid blue eye. She'd never felt more feminine or attractive. "Thank you."

He bowed over her hand, casting a swift, covert glance around. "I have a confession to make," he said playfully, straightening to his full, impressive height.

Peering up at him, she arched a skeptical brow. "Oh dear. Do I dare ask what?"

Who is this poised, flirtatious woman? Where'd

the dowdy, timid bird go?

As naturally as if they were old friends—no, no. Friends didn't go all quivery in their middles when they touched—Morgan cupped her elbow and drew her slightly to the side.

Not that he'd much space to do so, the room being packed with guests.

He bent his neck, and she couldn't haul her gaze from his.

"I might've, ah, altered the seating arrangements for dinner. And been caught in the act by our hosts' son. Allen kept watch at the dining room door until I finished." Up to his neckcloth in devilry, he grinned. Unrepentant, wholly boyish, and absolutely charming.

"And shall I approve of your presumptuousness, Captain?" Speaking of forwardness. From where had she summoned hers?

"You shall if you would enjoy sitting beside me." He cut an amused glance across the room. "Sterling might be miffed, however. You were to sit at his left."

Just as Alexa and Katrina glided into the room, absolutely ravishing in jeweled-toned gowns, Alexa's ruby and Katrina's sapphire, the dinner gong sounded. They gave her a little apologetic, fluttering finger wave as the guests sorted themselves into couples according to position and rank.

Lord Sterling gave her a lengthy, considering look before his attention shifted to Morgan. That same peculiar half-smile poised on his mouth, he extended his elbow to an elegant dame, dripping in jewels and layers of jonquil silk, and they led the dinner procession.

Shona let her fan slip from her hand then oh-so-casually toed it beneath an oval table nestled against the silk-papered wall.

"I've dropped my fan, Morgan."

Oh, well done you, Shona.

You slipped in the use of his name as naturally as if you are on the most intimate of terms.

And this, your very first attempt at feminine wiles.

A rousing success, I dare say.

She smiled up at him, and his sable brows climbed his forehead, his melodious chuckle pouring over her.

"So I see." He bent and, after retrieving the abused

accessory, passed it to her. "We'll be the last in."

She lifted a shoulder. "I wasn't walking in on Lord Glasscock's arm. He tries to look down my bosom and reeks of camphor. I'm afraid he intends to ask for my hand. Again."

"Again?"

"*Uh hum*. He's been most persistent since I came to London."

Morgan scratched his jaw. "Can't say I blame the aged codger."

Though his tone remained light, a steely undercurrent she couldn't identify seeped into his words.

Minutes later, he held her chair, and as she slipped onto the seat, Shona took quick inventory. The chair to her right hadn't been claimed, and she hadn't been introduced to the people directly across from her. The Harcourts and Pendergasts sat several places away to her left. Other than Lord Sterling across the table, and three chairs down, she'd never uttered a word to anyone near her.

Morgan gave the empty chair a perplexed,

considering look before he sank into his chair.

Someone bumped into her as they took their seat on her other side, and she automatically glanced over.

Her mouth went dry as pavement in August.

Mr. Le Draco snapped his serviette open, and as he placed it in his lap, gave her a frigid smile.

Her nape hairs froze in place at his glacial regard.

The lines of his face stony, his cool gaze cut to Morgan.

Tension radiated, hostile and intense, between the men.

Why, for all the saints in heaven, had Morgan seated her beside his father? The instinct to retreat into her diffident shell, to shyness's safety and familiarity, nearly suffocated her.

Morgan reached beneath the tablecloth and touched the back of her hand.

Despite her upset, a pleasurable jolt raced up her arm.

Taking a calming breath, she faced him, and he bent near her ear.

"He told me he was leaving after our quarrel, and I

haven't seen him since. I think he's only just come for dinner tonight. I swear, I wouldn't ever seat him beside you." The wrathful glance he fired his father would've sunk a schooner. "As much as I'm loath to admit it, his mind must've marched along the same path as mine, and he moved name cards."

"It's fine," she murmured.

Not really. Sitting beside the arctic man, disdain pulsing off him, she'd be fortunate if she didn't choke on her food.

"I'm quite accustomed to dealing with unpleasant parents," she said.

Truth there.

Och, crackers. She'd just called Morgan's father difficult. And what if Mr. Le Draco had heard her?

"We're much alike, it seems." The way Morgan said those five little words, his voice deep and husky, made her long to grab his hand, haul him into a dark nook, and beg him to kiss her.

What a wanton she'd become in mere days.

If anyone had told her a man she was newly acquainted with would have her throwing off a lifetime of restraints, taking risks she would've been petrified even to imagine before, she'd have called them daft or accused them of being foxed.

At this rate, with all the sensual yearnings Morgan had stirred, she'd be quite ruined before the week ended. Maybe that ought to have been her wager.

A wallflower's wonderfully wicked wager.

Despite the gravity of the situation, she quirked her mouth the teensiest bit.

An immaculately-attired footman served the soup, and Shona turned her attention to the meal. She lifted the spoon with her left hand, and a little thrill tiptoed from shoulder to waist when Morgan did as well.

Such an insignificant thing, perhaps, but one more they had in common.

Absorbed in her musings, trying to sort through her tumultuous feelings and determine what she should do about them, she ate in silence for several minutes.

Morgan seemed as disinclined to converse, though he did answer the questions put to him by the elderly dame seated on his other side.

Mr. Le Draco spoke not at all, but attended to his

food with gusto, accompanied by noisy slurping, chomping, and an occasional belch.

She peeked at him from beneath her lashes once and nearly dropped her fork to find him staring at her, his steely countenance all peeved angles and irritated planes.

Whyever was he vexed with her?

Over the course of the meal, she met Morgan's gaze several times. They also shared an equal number of polite smiles.

Something weary and haunting lingered in his.

By the time the final course was served, she and Morgan had exchanged short, mundane comments on every superficial topic from the stifling heat to the flower arrangements atop the table.

His father's presence cast a sobering ambiance—*more like a wet, smelly horse blanket*—on what she'd anticipated being an enjoyable affair.

She couldn't wait to escape his company.

The first slight bump to her arm Shona assumed accidental. After all, the table was crowded. However, the second, firmer nudge had been deliberate.

No doubt about it.

Nonetheless, she pretended absorption in her trifle.

She most definitely didn't want to talk to Mr. Le Draco, the odious man.

That day on the terrace, he'd looked at her like she was pond scum, and tonight, as if she were so far beneath his touch, he wanted to tread upon her as one would a bothersome insect.

A harder prod to her forearm couldn't be ignored.

Lips meshed into a thin hard line, she quickly scanned the guests to see if anyone had noticed.

A slight frown pulled Lord Sterling's dark brows together as he regarded Mr. Le Draco. He raised his unusual gray-green eyes to her, a question in their depths.

An astute man was Lord Sterling.

She managed a benign smile, despite fuming inwardly.

How dare Mr. Le Draco poke her like he was selecting ripe fruit from the market, the overbearing oaf? A gentleman would've addressed her, rather than treat her like a pin-cushion or ripe plum.

Summoning an indifferent expression, Shona peaked a brow and dispassionately met his gaze.

What?

"My son hasn't been able to find employment since his accident." He picked a piece of food from his teeth then studied the chunk of meat.

Barely refraining from skewing her mouth in distaste, she crumpled her napkin in a stranglehold instead.

Maybe she'd offer Morgan the stewardship position at Wedderford Abbey.

The delicious, oh-so-brilliant notion took hold, curling around her inside like a contented cat, lazing in the sun.

A perfect solution.

He required a position.

She required a bailiff.

And it was sure to infuriate his father.

All the more appealing.

"Morgan was supposed to take over my plantation for me. But it seems he's turned his sights on you instead." Hostile condescension riddled every brusque syllable.

She arched her brow higher.

Indeed?

How could this stony, calculating creature be Morgan's sire?

Mr. Le Draco raked his disapproving regard over her, lingering far too long on the swell of her breasts above her bodice. He scratched his hawkish nose, then yawned rudely.

"S'pose it's easier to marry money than earn it yourself."

8

Morgan jerked his head toward his father as Shona suppressed a gasp, her face draining of color.

Damn his eyes!

Morgan couldn't very well lean in front of her and tell his father to bugger off, the lying cur. Instead, he determined to redirect her attention before anyone else caught wind of the situation.

He'd deal with Father later.

Striving to control his ire, he spoke low to Shona. "Lady Atterberry, would you do me the honor of a stroll outdoors after dinner?"

Actually, he needed to get her alone, and after tolerating the fuggy dining room for upward of an hour, everyone was apt to stampede outside at the first opportunity.

Never mind that.

He knew the estate well, and a few secluded niches remained.

Hands folded primly in her lap, her confusion evident, she bit her lower lip.

He hated the leeriness that had crept into her big, soulful eyes. Loathed the splotches of scarlet on her cheekbones replacing the paleness Father's calculated words had caused.

Morgan dared catch her fingers in his beneath the tablecloth and give them a little reassuring press. "Please. I can explain. He's lying."

Her smile tremulous, she gave an infinitesimal nod. "I—"

Lady Wimpleton stood. "Ladies, shall we go through?"

Shona placed her serviette beside her plate, softly murmuring, "I'll meet you in the conservatory at half-past nine."

The flood of relief that washed over Morgan

should've worried him. He was too attached already, as improbable as that was. No good could come of continuing to spend time with Shona, and he'd been a selfish arse to ask her to this morning.

It wasn't fair to lead her on.

Others would echo Father's ugly accusation—at least the fortune-hunting part.

Instead, Morgan secretly rejoiced.

She'd agreed to see him alone.

He'd seize that crumb and cherish it.

Every bit the majestic lady, Shona didn't spare Father a glance as she departed, the Duchess of Harcourt on one side and the Duchess of Pendergast on the other.

Morgan leaned back in his chair and folded his arms. Through half-closed eyes, he regarded his father. "Your tactics won't work, you know. I'm not after her money. I'm well aware I have nothing worthy to offer, for which you are partially to blame."

Father shrugged, his smile just short of evil. "The gel doesn't know that. I've planted the suspicion. Now, she'll wonder if everything you do and say has an ulterior motive."

"Go. To. Hell." Morgan tossed his serviette on his plate and stood.

Fury tunneling through his veins, the truth of Father's words thundering in his head, he strode from the dining room. He didn't give a beggar's scorn that port and cigars followed dessert. If he didn't remove himself from Father's presence, he might well shuck any civility he yet possessed and lay him out.

Very real trepidation, worse than anything he'd experienced as a soldier, clawed at his lungs with each jagged breath he took.

Reaching inside his pocket for his watch, he cursed. He'd sold it two months ago.

Humiliating as hell to be in such damned low water. As he stalked down the corridor to the entry, he examined the longcase clock.

Over an hour 'til he met Shona.

If she showed up.

He wouldn't blame her if she didn't.

It wasn't fair or honorable to continue encouraging her. He'd rather lose his other eye than hurt her, but she'd sidled into his blood. No, she'd annihilated his carefully-erected ramparts and burrowed into the fortified shell he'd surrounded himself with.

Then she'd blinked those large, poignant eyes, and he was lost. She'd brought him more pleasure and optimism in the few days he'd known her than he'd ever anticipated experiencing again.

Yes, he was a selfish arse.

Yes, for her sake, he ought to pack his meager belongings and depart the house tonight, though God alone knew where he'd go.

And yes, he may very well regret this growing obsession—*probably would*—but much like an opium addict craving a pipe or a tippler hankering for a tot of whisky, Morgan ached for her company.

He yearned to see her winsome smile and the way her expressive, thick-lashed eyes lit with intelligence or radiated untainted joy. To hear her unusually low musical voice, the lyrical song of her rare laughter, to smell her delicious citrusy essence.

And when she gazed or peeked at him, shy and

adoring, as if he were a vanquishing hero slaying mythical dragons, he was willing to risk all. Him. A warped, beastly-faced man who never thought to have any woman look on him with such tenderness or desire again.

None of this made any bloody sense.

He would've laughed at and mocked another fellow in his situation.

Would've called him an addle-brained fool.

Morgan dreaded awaking and discovering this was all the dream of a disfigured man desperate for love and acceptance.

Pathetic and pitiable.

Glancing behind him, the quiet, empty corridor a gross misrepresentation of the house brimming with England's finest denizens, he blew out a deep breath.

To the lake then for a jot of peace and quiet. The exercise would also help alleviate his ire. Besides, he always ruminated better outdoors.

He let himself out the front entry, welcoming the slightly cooler temperature.

Dusk had fallen, and a few brave stars peeked out,

scouting the sky.

As Morgan tramped from the terrace, he automatically headed in the greenhouse's direction. He welcomed the gravel grinding beneath his heels, his irate steps echoing the litany of ugly thoughts cracking about in his head.

A person wasn't supposed to dislike his parents.

It went against nature.

Yet, the man Morgan had just left smirking at the table hadn't ever behaved like a loving, concerned father. It had taken Morgan years to understand the flaw was his father's, not his.

Shona, too, had suffered greatly because of a parent—her mother.

He'd had done a bit of sleuthing this afternoon. Finding the Duke of Harcourt in the stables, he'd introduced himself.

Morgan's lungs constricted, and his blood surged hotly once more when he recalled what the duke had told him about Shona's mother. No wonder she feared making mistakes.

Harcourt had said something else too. Something

that had given Morgan hope. Until Father opened his foul mouth at dinner and spewed his usual toxic poison.

"I knew Alexa was the woman for me the first time I laid eyes on her," Harcourt had said, stroking a bay's neck. He veered Morgan a sideways glance. "She was held captive in a Scottish fortress, and I helped rescue her." He grinned, pointing to his eye. "She punched me."

Morgan had laughed, automatically touching his eye patch.

"She packed quite a wallop too, I tell you."

"Your Grace, might I ask why you're telling me this?" Morgan hadn't been sure what to expect from the infamous Duke of Harcourt, but a cordial discussion, a personal conversation, hadn't topped the list.

Harcourt stopped petting the horse and angled his head the merest bit, his expression inscrutable.

"Shona deserves happiness." Notching a shoulder upward, he scratched his eyebrow. "She's of age, so I don't really have a say in what she does. But, I won't stand in the way if you wish to court her." His tone became unyielding iron. "However, hear me well. You hurt her, and you'll answer to me. I'm a powerful man, Le Draco. One you do not want to cross."

A blessing and a threat in the same sentence.

Still, that chat had lit a scrap of hope in Morgan, albeit a miniscule one. And that confidence had grown when Shona had been so endearingly obvious in the drawing room. Father's rancor had doused Morgan's spark of optimism as efficiently as a bucket of water poured over a candle.

He meant to eschew the conservatory for his favorite nook at the lake, but as he passed, barely audible weeping filtered from inside, and he automatically glanced through the open doors.

A woman, her back to the door, sat hunched on the bench, her face in her palms. Every now and again, her shoulders trembled when she took an uneven breath.

Shona.

Rage toward his father pummeled Morgan.

Treading softly, he approached her.

Consumed with her heartache, she didn't hear him

until he was nearly upon her.

She jumped to her feet, her eyes wide and frightened, clasping her throat with one hand. Visibly relaxing when she recognized Morgan, leeriness promptly replaced her relief. Averting her head and angling her back to him, she swiped at her eyes.

"What are you doing here? I said I'd meet you at half-past nine." Her voice, low and throaty from crying, tore at his already bleeding heart.

"I was on my way to the lake when I heard you weeping." He touched her arm, and when she didn't pull away, he cupped her shoulders and gently turned her until she faced him. "Why are you crying?"

Chin tucked to her chest, she shook her head, the pert curls around her face brushing her cheeks. A ragged breath juddered through her. She stood there so dejected, so broken, and he ached for her.

With his crooked forefinger, Morgan tilted her chin upward.

Tears yet glistened in her forlorn eyes, darker than a moonless night at the moment, and marked uncertainty bracketed her mouth.

"You can tell me, Shona. Is it because of the codswallop my father told you?"

A fresh tear leaked from the corner of one eye, and she shifted her gaze away. "It's nothing," she whispered, blinking several times. "I've just been foolish. That's all."

Such stoicism. How often had she blamed herself for others' poor behavior?

Despite the impropriety, he drew her to his chest, one hand cradling her spine and the other her face. He spoke into the fine hairs over her ear. "How so?"

She was all soft womanly curves, and her every contour fit tidily into his body. Never had holding a female felt so right. And she didn't flinch from him, didn't seem to care in the least that he was unsightly.

Except for the fountain's comforting, rhythmic splashing and an occasional sleepy bird's call, silence reigned. Heavy and sorrowful.

An uninvited thought battered him.

Had Father destroyed Morgan's one chance at love?

Shona remained still for so long, he didn't think

she intended to answer. Which meant his father had indeed caused her tears, God rot the selfish bugger.

Father's actions tonight were the proverbial final straw. Time to sever the relationship. Permanently. Viola was all that had kept Morgan from doing so years before.

He sighed into Shona's silky hair, the scent he'd come to associate with her filling his nostrils. Orange blossoms. Fresh and entrancing. And sweet, like her, with a hint of what he thought might be cloves. Fitting since he suspected she had a spicy side to her nature.

He brushed her head with his cheek. "It's all right, Shona. You don't have to tell me. I think I know."

"Nae, ye dinnae."

An unbidden smile bent his mouth at her slip into Scots. The blunder showed just how discomfited she truly was.

Morgan waited. He'd not pressure her. He bloody well knew what it was like to be harangued incessantly.

She absently toyed with his lapel. Likely wasn't even aware she fiddled with it.

He rejoiced that she was so comfortable in his presence that she'd take such a liberty.

Her shoulders slumped as she released a lengthy sigh.

"I'd thought I could change. That I could stop being a dowdy, mousy thing. An object of scorn." She looked over his shoulder, her pretty mouth pulled into a rueful line. She glanced up before her spikey-lashed gaze danced away. "I'd determined that instead of dreading this week, and eagerly waiting for it to end, I'd enjoy myself. And I could do that because I thought you—"

She swallowed and lifted a shoulder an inch, averting her gaze once more.

"Shona, my father lied. I'm an abolitionist, and since I was eighteen, I've refused to oversee his slave plantations. I am in need of employment, that's true. But only because my father resigned my commission while I was recuperating."

Her pretty mouth tightened in disapproval. "That was awful of him."

'Awful' pretty much described Ruben Le Draco.

"I've been seeking a position." Without any luck so far. "I swear, my interest has nothing whatsoever to do with your title or fortune." Morgan brushed the back of his hand across her soft cheek. "I shall confess, however, I felt something pass between us the instant our eyes met."

She stopped fidgeting with his lapel, then hesitantly raised her gaze to his. "I felt it too, Morgan." A wisp of color flared across her face at her bold declaration. "A strange, prickling sensation," she whispered. "It caused my heart to beat strangely and my breath to catch."

He'd suspected she had, but her scintillating, naïve admission sent his soul soaring.

He searched her face.

The invitation was there, in her eyes. Innocent and wary, and so uncertain. Fear tinged the edges too. Dread of rejection and scorn, he'd wager. What suffering her generous spirit must have endured.

Framing her silky jaw with his hand, he angled her head as he lowered his. Inch by agonizingly slow inch, he dipped lower, giving her time to pull away.

She remained statue-like, frozen in place. Neither retreating nor encouraging him. Desire warred with apprehension in the depths of her eyes.

"Shona, I want to kiss you. But I won't if that's not what you want too."

Her focus strayed to his mutilated mouth, and she reverently outlined his lips with her fingertip. She alone made him feel whole again. As if the ugly, puckered ridges didn't matter.

"I want to kiss you too, Morgan. I don't know how, though. I've never been kissed."

Such frankness and transparency splayed his heart wide open.

He kissed the end of her nose. "I'll teach you. It's not that difficult."

The force of her incandescent smile plowed into him with the power of a pair of draft horses.

Going slow with this tempting armful would be hellish.

She licked the seam of her mouth with her small tongue, and he checked the groan billowing from his chest.

Almost.

Drawing her closer, giving her time to adjust to being embraced, he nuzzled her ear, before gently nipping her earlobe.

Another sigh whispered past her parted lips as she instinctively angled her neck to allow him better access. Then she balanced on her toes and touched her mouth to his. The sweetest, tentative feathering.

He let her set the pace, though passion thrummed through him, a jubilant fanfare of longing. And a glorious, humbling triumph that she trusted him. Desired him.

Making an inarticulate sound in the back of her throat, she threaded her fingers through his hair. Her breath coming in short, excited pants, she pressed her mouth harder to his.

Holding his passion strictly in control took every ounce of Morgan's will. His starving body yearned to yank her to him and sample every inch of her voluptuous form, starting with her glorious breasts. With his tongue, he plied the corners of her mouth until she yielded, her lips parting like the dewy petals of a rose.

He swept her mouth with his tongue, fire igniting in his blood.

"God, Shona. You taste so sweet."

Shona gripped the back of Morgan's head with one hand, the other fisted in his coat, else she'd have sagged at his feet. Never could she have dreamed a kiss would send her veins to singing, her head to spinning, and turn her muscles to jelly.

Nestled against his firm, molded body, she strained to get closer.

Like a man long-starved, he devoured her mouth. He pressed hot kisses to her eyes, her cheeks, and her chin before claiming her mouth again.

And she relished, rejoiced in every moment. She'd suspected his kisses would be spectacular. Had craved his mouth upon hers since he'd helped her from the lake and her senses had become alert in a carnal way she'd never experienced before.

The hardened patch on his lip from his scar only increased her desire. She wanted to comfort him and greedily seize everything he was teaching her and commit the wonder to memory.

Och. Such a delicious thing to have wished. To have wagered—a kiss from Captain Morgan Le Draco. But now she feared—*nae, kent*—it wasn't enough.

She wanted more. So much more. More than she had any right to dream of.

He shifted her slightly so that she rested in the crook of his arm, cradled against his shoulder. His sizzling gaze scorched her, and her unbridled desire welled higher yet. Confident and sure, his exploration trailed lower, down her neck, the juncture of her throat. Then lower still, until he grazed his lips across the swell of her breasts.

"Morgan," she breathed, bowing into him.

"I love it when you say my name, darling. Your husky voice drives me mad for want of you."

He settled one big hand on her breast, and she gasped.

Laughter rang from outside, intruding on the magical moment.

"Devil a bit." Morgan gave her a swift, hard kiss on the mouth. "The other guests seek respite from the stuffy house too. I can't be found here with you. We must consider your repute."

"I don't care. I'm not ashamed to be with you."

And Shona wasn't. She was proud and honored that such a noble man found her desirable.

More laughter carried across the greens.

Good heavens.

Had everyone on the guest list decided to parade about in the growing dusk?

"You don't know how happy that makes me, Shona, my heart. But I won't have your name on the gable grinders' tongues." He shot a swift glance behind him. "I'll leave through the other door." His tender gaze pouring over her face, a potent caress, he seized her hands and fervently kissed the knuckles. "Until tomorrow, my sweet."

"Yes. Until tomorrow." Shona smiled and touched his dear face. "Morgan, wait. My estate, Wedderford

Abbey, has need of a steward. The position is yours if you want it."

"I'd be honored, but we'll have to discuss it later. I must be off, else your reputation will suffer." With a smoldering smile and a devilish wink, he disappeared out the opening.

A fortune-hunter would've stayed. Would've seized the opportunity to see her compromised. His departure spoke to his credible character and vaulted him even higher in her estimation.

Scant moments after Morgan left, a score of guests sauntered into the greenhouse. Most, after giving her a cursory glance, wandered to other parts of the conservatory, except Miss Rossington and her two ever-present lackeys.

Those hellions made straight for Shona, standing beside the bench.

Thunder and turf. Not that trio again.

Were there tear tracks on her face still? Were her lips berry-red from Morgan's kisses?

"We wondered where you'd disappeared to after dinner, Lady Atterberry," Miss Rossington said, while the Dundercroft sisters giggled like simpkins and nudged each other.

I'll just bet you did.

"I felt a trifle unwell, and thought the fresh air might do me good."

Mr. Le Draco's hateful words had sickened her to her soul, truth to tell.

Shona retrieved her discarded gloves, and after draping one over her forearm, offered a genuine smile as she drew the other onto her fingers. Miss Rossington wouldn't rob her of the last few minutes' marvelousness. "Please excuse me."

"You're alone?" Miss Rossington made an exaggerated pretense of scrutinizing the greenhouse before her deprecating gaze settled on Shona once more. "I'd thought perhaps you'd arranged a *tête-à-tête.*" The incredulity in her voice suggested she thought no such thing. "In an attempt to win our private wager."

I already won.

Miss Rossington blinked innocently and, pressing her fingertips to her mouth, tittered as if she'd revealed an immense secret.

The knowledge that Shona had shared several glorious kisses with Morgan was a tremendous boost to her self-assurance. Nevertheless, she had no intention of revealing something so special to this nit simply to win a silly bet.

Shona made to move past. "I suppose you'll never know, will you?"

"Does that mean she's already kissed someone, Francine?" Eyes rounding in confusion, Miss Lyselle tugged on her sister's arm. "But…" she spluttered. "But Penelope said no man would—"

"Be quiet, Lyselle," Miss Rossington ordered, her cat-like green eyes narrowed into a withering glare.

Here come the claws.

"Lady Atterberry, may I escort you back to the house?" a man's deep voice intoned.

Shona swiveled toward the baritone, as did a few of the others enjoying the greenhouse.

Lord Sterling ambled in the other entrance, his shoes striking a sharp staccato on the floor. He swept Miss Rossington an unperturbed, dismissive look.

Shona's pulse slowed before quickening in alarm.

Had he seen Morgan leave?

Would he say anything if he had?

What did it matter?

She wasn't ashamed. Every moment she'd spent in Morgan's embrace had been a wondrous gift.

Mustering her composure, she finished putting on her other glove. She offered a grateful smile as she laid her fingertips on his extended arm. "I would appreciate it, my lord."

Perceptive man. He'd promptly determined the delicacy of the situation and provided Shona a pride-saving escape. He seemed in the habit of rescuing her from Penelope Rossington.

Miss Rossington's gaze swung between Lord Sterling and Shona, animosity sparking in her eyes. She stepped nearer Shona, and making no effort to temper her volume, accused, "You *did* arrange a tryst."

Several nearby guests swung their attention toward them, their avid gazes alight with uncensored curiosity.

Well into a dust-up now, Miss Rossington seemed

to have forgotten they weren't alone. Or perhaps—*likely*—that was her intention.

To try to humiliate Shona.

She bit her lower lip, then straightened her spine. She wasn't allowing bullying poltroons like Penelope Rossington to intimidate her anymore.

Chin quavering and venom dripping from each hissed word, Miss Rossington pointed an unsteady finger at Lord Sterling. "You arranged an assignation with Lord Sterling, didn't you?" On the verge of tears, she shook her shiny blond head, her diamond and pearl earrings bobbing with the frenetic motion. "I don't know how *you* could've possibly enticed him. He's ignored my—"

"Quite so," Lord Sterling snapped, his eyes jade shards, and his countenance as unyielding as marble.

Oh, dear.

Shona cast him a sympathetic glance.

So Miss Rossington had thought to sink her sharpened claws into his lordship, and he'd rebuffed her. Fortunate for him. He was much too decent and kind-hearted a man to suffer the misfortune of taking a selfish shrew like Miss Rossington to wife.

"But, Penelope, you said Lord Sterling held a *tendre* for *you*." Her chuffy face growing redder by the moment, Lyselle's forehead crumpled in befuddlement. "I don't understand. Why would he—?"

Dense as London's pea soup fog.

"Shut up, Lyselle!" Miss Rossington snarled, all pretense of civility gone. Holding her arms akimbo, her irate gaze circled the hothouse, beckoning everyone to heed her.

Shona cringed inwardly as person after person trained their enthralled gaze upon them.

"I don't know how she managed it, but this Scottish dumpling," Miss Rossington waved her hand wildly as if batting at a pesky fly, "was alone with a man in this very conservatory. Doing only God knows what. Given her flushed cheeks and swollen mouth, I think we can draw our own conclusions."

Och, Guid.

Shona balled her hands to keep from slapping her palms to her burning face and giving more credence to Miss Rossington's ugly—*true*—allegation.

"Perhaps, Miss Rossington, your blind jealousy clouds your inability to acknowledge Lady Atterberry's loveliness," Lord Sterling said.

At his compliment, Shona gaped. He'd never hinted he found her attractive.

Under his scathing contempt, Miss Rossington's face reddened to the tips of her glowing ears.

However, Lord Sterling wasn't finished with his scold. "But more on point, and of far greater concern, is the disservice you do Lady Atterberry by publicly inferring she participates in the same manner of sordid dalliances you are known to."

At his blatant disdain, Miss Rossington went white as the pearls at her slender throat. She opened and closed her mouth thrice, giving her the unfortunate appearance of a dying fish.

By now, everyone remaining in the conservatory had stilled to listen to the titillating conversation. Agog, a concert of gazes trained on the unfolding scene, they made no pretense otherwise.

Never comfortable as the center of attention, Shona wanted nothing more than to disappear. His chivalrous defense wouldn't put to rest Miss Rossington's vile accusation entirely.

"Shall we go, my lady?" Lord Sterling jutted his chin in the door's direction. "Before I forget I'm a gentleman?"

Francine Dundercroft marched to her friend's side, and after wrapping a comforting arm about Miss Rossington's waist, glowered at Shona. "I hope you're happy, you … you neep." She angled her head haughtily. "Winning your vulgar wager to snare a lord for a lover this week has broken another's heart."

9

Morgan had hoped he'd see Shona at breakfast again today. Luck wasn't with him, however. He prowled about the house for the next pair of hours, even declining a much-coveted ride with Wimpleton just so he might encounter her.

When the clock chimed eleven, and she'd yet to make an appearance, his jubilation from last night ebbed, replaced with an ominous sense of foreboding.

Finally, after finding a fifth flimsy excuse to wander past the stairway, floral salon, and drawing room—after covertly peeking in the library, music and dining rooms, and strolling around the entire house's perimeter, twice—he caught sight of Harcourt in an earnest conversation with Sterling near the stables.

A picnic was scheduled for midday on a nearby knoll, and Morgan happily anticipated sharing a blanket with Shona. Especially since he'd learned his father had departed Davenswood after dinner, and he needn't fear another unpleasant episode like last night.

Perhaps she was unwell.

Had she taken a chill from her dip in the lake after all?

Or was she suffering qualms about kissing him?

The latter thought left a bitter taste in his mouth and caused an even more acrid pang to his soul.

Not wishing to intrude upon Harcourt and Sterling's privacy, but hopeful the duke might have knowledge of Shona's whereabouts or condition if she were indeed indisposed, he pretended absorption in the potted topiaries and statuary adoring the terrace's other side as he waited for their conversation to end.

A cluster of women shared two benches paralleling the veranda, a tidy hornbeam hedge creating a partition between the chatting gaggle and Morgan.

He gave them a dismissive glance as he strolled

by. Once behind the greenery, he couldn't see the ladies any longer, though their subdued conversation carried to him.

"The silly chit got herself compromised last night," one lady said, no trace of mercy in her pompous tone.

"I don't believe it," another argued in an incredulous whisper. "She's so bashful. Why, in London, she couldn't even string two words together when a gentleman came near."

"I was in the conservatory, and I tell you, it is so," the first chinwag insisted. "His lordship did not deny he was her lover, either. Seems terribly unfair the likes of *her* making such a credible match."

"Well, she entrapped him, naturally. How else could someone like her have managed such a coup? And his honor has always been above reproach." A breathy sigh flitted through the hedgerow. "Such a waste of a title."

Had the jealous hens nothing better to do than bandy about some poor woman's unfortunate, and no doubt highly exaggerated, circumstance?

Fool. Of course not. These fine citizens live to shred another's character.

Rubbing his forehead above his eye patch—it ached bloody awful today—Morgan scanned the lawns again in search of Shona.

Harcourt and Sterling, still deep in discussion, wandered toward the manor.

Hands on his hips, his brows pulled into a slight crease, Morgan shook his head then made to go inside once more. He'd taken but two steps when one of the nattering women's next word yanked him to an abrupt halt, mid-step.

"I also heard, straight from Miss Rossington herself, that Lady Atterberry wagered her she could engage a lover for the week," a third voice intoned, this one squeaky with unsuppressed glee. "Who'd have thought *that* wallflower would've succeeded so quickly? And with such a fine specimen of manhood too?"

Jerking his head so that his good ear was toward them, Morgan edged closer, unabashedly eavesdropping

"That's not how it was at all," another, kinder voice objected. "I was told she wagered she'd get herself kissed before the week was out. And she only did so, because, cruel as always, Penelope said no man would ever want to kiss Lady Atterberry."

Is that what Shona had whispered to the pernicious virago?

Suspicion uncoiled, raising its serpent's chary head. He'd thought she'd whispered a proper set down to the chit.

Is that why Shona had kissed him? To win a preposterous wager?

He would've rather believed maidenly curiosity prompted her than an ulterior motive.

No. What he wanted to believe—needed to believe—was that she'd been as fraught to feel her mouth against his as he'd been to taste the velvety softness of her lips.

And who was this gentleman she'd been found with?

How could she possibly have been compromised?

Morgan had barely exited the greenhouse before

the throng entered. True, he hadn't loitered, but had sought the lake as he'd originally intended. It was possible another had entered after him.

Fabric rustled as one lady stood, her yellow-ribboned straw bonnet covering a cloud of brilliant red hair.

Olivia Wimpleton, Allen's wife.

Morgan darted behind a statue of ... Zeus? Apollo?

He had no idea who the god was or if he was Roman or Greek, but the sculptor had been rather—er, extremely—generous with the deity's manly endowments.

And bloody hell. Why was he skulking behind statuary like an errant schoolboy?

"I've heard all the ridiculous twaddle I can tolerate. I refuse to sit here and listen to you malign Lady Atterberry's character an instant longer. Smudging the sweet-tempered girl's reputation." Mrs. Wimpleton shook her head as she angled her parasol over her shoulder. "I simply cannot credit any of you with such unkindness. She's been nothing but pleasant to each of you. Her life has not been easy. In fact, three years ago, she missed her come-out because her mother beat her so badly. You ought to be ashamed, bandying about such fustian rubbish."

My God. Her mother had beat Shona that severely?

"Olivia, is it true that Lord Sterling actually asked for her hand last night? He's speaking with her guardian yonder even now."

Sterling had offered for Shona?

The buzzing in Morgan's head, as if a myriad of bees swarmed within his skull, several stabbing his aching head with their stingers, made it impossible to decipher which woman had asked the question.

The humming grew louder, muting Mrs. Wimpleton's response.

He shook his head, then cursed as thundering pain lanced his skull, threatening to split it in two. If he had an ounce of sense, he'd seek his bed until the throbbing ceased.

Pressing a hand to his pulsating forehead, he caught sight of the marquis.

With every fiber of his being, Morgan wanted to hate Sterling.

But truth be told, he was exactly the sort of chap Shona deserved.

An honorable man, not given to any vices, a veritable pinnacle of propriety. Not to mention wealthy and too blasted handsome for his own good. Perhaps a jot too serious for her, but Morgan didn't harbor a doubt that Sterling would treat her well. Reverently even.

There'd been a hungry glint in his eye when he'd gazed at her yesterday.

Morgan ought to have recognized the look, for no doubt a matching gleam shone in his.

At the very least, Sterling found her attractive, but Morgan suspected something more lay in the marquis's appreciative gaze.

Sterling cared for her.

Shona would be foolish not to accept.

Had she accepted already?

That would explain her absence—she probably didn't want to face Morgan or endure the telling glances and whispers of the other guests.

Except, despite obviously being a sensitive soul, a thread of courage pumped through her veins. He'd seen the merest trace himself, and if nurtured, Shona would eventually cast off her shell of diffidence and blossom into a truly exquisite flower.

Only he wouldn't be the man to bring about the transformation.

He shot Harcourt and Sterling another glance.

They shook hands and laughed, then Harcourt slapped Sterling on the shoulder before changing direction and striding toward the manor's front.

Morgan's lungs cramped so tight he fought to draw in a steadying breath.

Suddenly, he had to be alone.

Had to have time to process this blow.

Stupid idiot. Fool. Imbecile.

He'd permitted his emotions free rein and look where that had landed him. Halfway—hell, there was no halfway about it—in love with a woman too far above him.

Impossible to fall in love in such a short time.

How many times had he contemptuously uttered those very words?

How Fate must be laughing at him now. Bent double, howling with glee.

A disgusted half-snort, half-laugh escaped him as he strode toward the oak grove.

Why wouldn't Shona choose Sterling over him? The marquis was everything Morgan wasn't.

The day promised to be every bit as warm as yesterday, and perspiration beaded his face at his frenzied pace across the greens. Staying for the rest of the house party was impossible now.

Head lowered, hands entwined behind his back, he slowed his gait once he entered the oaks' leafy covering. Swallowing against the bitter disappointment burning his throat, he lifted his aching head and gazed at the lake, a million diamonds reflecting off the pristine waters.

He'd tasted a bit of heaven, had embraced hope for a few glorious hours.

Now, he must decide where to go.

America, perhaps.

As Morgan emerged through the oaks, Shona straightened on the natural seat the trunks growing together had created. She'd removed her bonnet and gloves again. It seemed she was destined to breach protocol.

At Wedderford, she never intended to wear either.

Well, only when she absolutely must.

Head bowed, her rugged, broad-shouldered, brave warrior appeared so dejected. So lost.

Morgan had heard the ugly tattle, of course.

How could he not with the house full of people eager to blather the latest *on dit*?

For the first time in years, she'd cried herself to sleep, waking with puffy eyes and despondency shrouding her.

Absently grazing her hand over the rough trunk, she permitted herself the luxury of scouring him with her gaze. Every precious detail, every dear nuance, she committed to memory.

His overly long hair, tied at his nape; the strength of his powerful form; his big hands, balled into fists. His long, muscled legs, braced as he gazed at the lake. Everything about him called to her on a primal level she didn't even attempt to analyze.

She wanted to be with him. As simple as that.

When she was in his presence, she felt complete.

It didn't matter that she'd known him mere days.

If she were the fanciful sort, given to believing romantic nonsense, she might be persuaded to believe she'd found her soul mate. That instant recognition one spirit has when it encounters the one meant to meld with theirs.

A few days ago, she'd have dismissed such thoughts as nonsensical twaddle. Today, however…

Before most of the guests had even awoken, she'd sneaked out here. Unwilling to skulk in her chamber—after all, she hadn't done what she'd been accused of—she wasn't prepared to endure the other guests' speculative glances or probing questions at breakfast either.

Mostly, she'd fretted about Morgan's reaction.

Surely he wouldn't believe the lie.

Why not? Everyone else had.

Except her family.

Last night had gone from unbearably joyful to wholly horrific in just a few short moments.

Once Francine Dundercroft's vile accusation pealed through the conservatory with the intensity of Notre Dame's clanging bells in a linen closet, the guests had either dived together to chatter in sotto voce whispers or scurried like cockroaches to share the succulent tidbit.

By the time Lord Sterling had steered Shona into the house, Alexa and Harcourt, along with the Needhams and the Pendergasts had been waiting to whisk them into the library.

Her stomach toppled again in remembrance.

Morgan rubbed his nape and, heaving a sigh that lifted his shoulders, angled toward the alcove.

He stopped short upon spotting her.

No rakish tilt of his lips or engaging spark in his eye greeted her this time. His expression slammed closed as surely as a shutter yanked across a window.

Then was locked securely.

A man who'd retreated into his carefully-constructed fortress.

A man accustomed to protecting himself from hurt.

The man she loved.

His stance cautious and gaze hooded, he regarded her. Silent. Pensive.

Yet, tenderness softened the corners of his eye.

"Hello, Morgan."

Shona could've pinched herself.

What a daft, fumbling, inept thing to say.

Couldn't she have come up with something more poignant? Even forward or fast?

Such as, *Even though I saw you less than twelve hours ago, I've missed you terribly?*

Don't believe the lies you've heard.

There's only one man I ever want to kiss me.

You.

She'd been wishing he'd appear. Had chosen this spot hoping he would and had almost given up when hours had passed and he hadn't come.

"I understand congratulations are in order." His deep voice, so warm and velvety yesterday, had gone stiff and formal. Raw and cracked around the outside as if he struggled to present an unaffected front.

Her soul wept for him. Felt the pain radiating from him.

Running her fingertip along her bonnet's brim, she shook her head. "Nothing's been decided yet."

Lord Sterling would make a wonderful husband.

The type she'd never even permitted herself to imagine offering for her. Drab brown wrens didn't catch the regard of the likes of the Marquis of Sterling.

She'd nearly fallen off the settee when he'd offered for her right there and then last night. The words flowing so smoothly and confidently and sincerely she almost believed he'd rehearsed them many times.

And he hadn't seemed all that miffed about asking for her hand under the humiliating circumstances. She'd known him to be an honorable man, but sacrificing himself to the parson's mousetrap over a silly chit's jealous drivel seemed excessive, even to

Shona.

She'd seriously contemplated escaping to Wedderford Abbey at dawn, both to relieve Lord Sterling of his misplaced obligation and to save herself a great deal of discomfort.

But to never see Morgan again?

To not explain and pray he'd listen? Pray that he also wanted to pursue whatever this magnetism was between them?

Nae. That she couldn't bear.

The unexpected reaction from Alexa and the others further complicated matters. They believed a match with Lord Sterling something Shona ought to give a good deal of careful consideration to. And toward that end, they'd all agreed to wait and discuss the matter further after the house party.

Before meeting Morgan, Shona most probably would've accepted Lord Sterling's offer.

However, now she much preferred to marry another.

Even though the man of her choice had never hinted at any such thing. Hadn't known her long enough to.

"I've been asked to carefully consider the match," she said.

Morgan relaxed the merest bit, bending one knee and cocking his head. "You will accept Sterling."

It sounded like an order he expected obeyed. Inarguable. Irrefutable.

Her hackles rose at his assumption that she'd acquiesce.

"He's your social equal and a man of stellar repute." Jaw flexing, Morgan pointed his attention to the branches overhead.

Why wouldn't he look at her?

Just what was he about?

His acceptance of the situation and encouragement to accept Lord Sterling, corroded her newly-acknowledged love.

"He'll treat you well, of that I have no doubt," Morgan murmured, almost as if speaking to himself. As if he tried to convince himself of that truth. "You'll never want for anything."

Except the man my heart has decided to love.

"It's not a decision I'll be rushed into making. There is much to consider. Wedderford Abbey, for one. I don't want to relinquish the entire running of the estate to someone else, for I'm certain Lord Sterling would prefer to reside in England. Besides, as I mentioned last night, I've no agent at present."

Preposterous to assume Morgan would consider the stewardship. Not now. Just as ludicrous to presume she'd accept Lord Sterling's offer. Knowing another held her affections, it would be unfair to him. She might've been happy with him had she not toppled into the lake and fallen in love with her rescuer.

"Surely Harcourt knows of someone capable." Morgan turned that one startling blue eye on her, and even the corners of his dear face creased with tense resignation. "You must realize I cannot accept the position."

No surprise there, yet regret still caused strange, prickly spasms behind her ribs.

After setting her bonnet and gloves aside, Shona stood. "As the duke is no longer my guardian, it isn't his concern."

He made a rough sound of disagreement in the back of his throat. His knitted chestnut brows, and the fingertips he drummed against his thigh revealed his preoccupation. He pulled at his waistcoat, the most insecure she'd ever seen him.

A bit of oak moss dropped from the tree and landed on her shoulder. As she brushed the lichen away, she cocked her head. Did she dare voice the thoughts swirling 'round and 'round in her mind?

What did she have to lose?

"Although I cannot argue against any of the things you've said about Lord Sterling, I do not love him."

"You might come to in time." Morgan cut her a glance she couldn't quite decipher. "In any event, some things are more important than love."

Marshaling her courage, she gave him a crooked, far-from-confident smile and shook her head. "Not to me. You see, I've craved unconditional love my entire life."

He might as well know the whole of it. Know her deepest secrets.

Why love someone if you couldn't risk

vulnerability with them?

"Through my darkest trials, when I was starved, beaten, my arm broken once, locked in my chamber—for weeks on end, at times—I yearned to be loved. When my mother tried to force me to marry one wealthy, revolting codger after another, even when I realized she was stark mad and plotting to kill my sister, I held on to the feeble hope that someday, someone would cherish me. Accept me just the way I am."

She gestured dismissively at the front of her Pomona green gown, her voice thick with the sincerity of her emotional declaration.

"It's all that kept me going."

"Shona…"

"There's nothing, *nothing,* Morgan, I wouldn't forsake or sacrifice for someone I love—*for you*— if he loved me in return."

He made another rough, gravelly sound in his throat and shut his eye, his lashes a thick sable fan across his suntanned cheekbone. "I would gladly do the same. Only, I haven't anything of value worth sacrificing."

He opened his eye, such stark pain lining his face that she wanted to run to him, wrap her arms around his strong, sturdy form, and tell him how very wrong he was. The love of such a noble man, if she dared believe he might love her, was all she would ever need to be content for the rest of her days.

"I've nothing to offer a woman either," he said, so low his lips scarcely moved. "Except a face so ravaged, children cry out and cringe in fear when they see me."

Our children wouldn't.

The unbidden thought jolted her clear to her toes then sent a frisson scampering back up her spine, causing her nape hairs to twitch in excitement.

As if chagrined by his confession, he turned abruptly and took a couple of lengthy strides away.

"Oh, Morgan," Shona whispered, compassion for his suffering tangling her insides. "Your face, even scarred, is more precious to me than any other man's unflawed features could ever be."

Love emboldened her to speak her mind. Perhaps

imprudently, she acknowledged as she clasped her hands until her fingertips grew numb, the silence stretching taut and awkward between them. Every passing second doused her hope like water droplets steadily dripping onto a dying fire's embers.

He heaved a throaty sigh and scraped his hand through his hair, pulling several strands free of the ribbon at his nape. "I should return to the house. I've no wish to cause a rift between you and Sterling, nor provide more *on dit* for the gossips. I'm leaving as soon as I've packed."

Why did he continue to insist there was, or could be, anything between her and Lord Sterling?

Morgan was the one who said she had expressive eyes. Couldn't he see the love glowing in them for him?

He smiled, a tender, sad, defeated thing, the uninjured side of his mouth not quite bending. "Shona, I wish—"

Giving an infinitesimal shake of his head, he pressed his lips into a severe line, causing his scar to stand out, stark and white. A jagged, cruel testament to his inner turmoil. However, his tender gaze caressed her as surely as if he'd brushed his big, callused hand over her bare flesh.

Desire flared, immediate and potent.

In that instant, Shona knew. She almost gasped at her sudden insight. Morgan *was* making love's supreme sacrifice for her. By encouraging her to marry Lord Sterling, a man he believed could provide her with everything he could not.

Foolish, dear man.

And if she let him walk away without telling him how she felt, let her innate bashfulness and fear of rejection keep her from declaring her love, she'd never forgive herself. She'd live with the regret for the rest of her life.

She came to him, and after taking his scarred hand in hers, kissed the back of it, where fine dark hairs covered the sun-browned flesh.

His features grew even more guarded, but he didn't pull away.

She pressed his hand to her face and rubbed her cheek against the warm, solid flesh. Raising her gaze, she murmured, "I love you, Morgan. And I don't want to marry anyone else."

If she'd expected him to grin or whoop for joy, to declare his love and sweep her into his arms and shower her with passionate kisses, she was very much mistaken.

He gently withdrew his hand, his expression inscrutable. "I am deeply honored, and your words humble me, but they change nothing."

Had she played her hand too soon?

Played the wrong hand entirely?

Had her newly dredged up boldness backfired?

She searched his face, desperate to find a trace of the desire she'd seen yesterday. The minutest flicker of the silver flecks in his eye encouraged her.

"You are wrong. I've prayed for a man like you my whole life. I know we met but a few days ago, and I won't pretend to understand how it happened. But love doesn't adhere to a watch or a calendar, Morgan. Love can happen in an instant."

He remained silent, yet she pressed onward.

"Maybe not for everyone. It may take some longer

for their affection to grow. Others don't recognize the sentiment for what it is at first. But you and I…" She gestured between them, her voice growing strong, more confident. "When our eyes met as you swam across the lake to me, I felt my heart open."

Like a rosebud waiting for the sun's warming rays.

"Don't. It's impossible." Voice raw and rough, he tucked his head to his chest, posture rigid and fists clenched at his sides

It took a fraction for her to understand.

He wept.

This brave, wounded soldier cried because she'd declared her affection. And she hadn't a doubt, he'd been as ravenous, as fraught for her love as she was for his.

She could have no more stopped herself from twining her arms about his waist, laying her head against his shuddering chest, and holding him tight than she could've saved herself from the lake that day.

"All I want is you, Morgan. If you'll have me. If you love me, it *is* enough."

Slowly, as if waking from a trance, he encircled her with his strong arms and pulled her nearer. So close not a hair's breadth separated them.

"People will say that I'm a fortune-hunter."

"Are you?"

Of course he wasn't, but somehow, she knew he needed to tell her so himself.

His breath warmed her scalp as he pressed his lips to her crown. "No. If you had nothing but the clothes on your back," he gave her a squeeze, "which by the way, you look exceedingly fetching in today, I'd grovel at your feet for a kind word. Still, the tongue-waggers will spread ugly tales. It cannot be helped."

She shook her head against his chest and chuckled. "Pooh. My mother's a convicted criminal and your father's a slave-owner. Both are far more offensive than pretentious people judging us. Besides, you're forgetting just how powerful my brother-in-law is. And he has loads of equally powerful friends."

"Are you sure, Shona? Absolutely sure? You've no doubt whatsoever?" He held her snugger, as if afraid she'd change her mind. "What's happened between us is irregular. I couldn't bear for you to decide you'd made an impulsive mistake later on."

He certainly sounded like a man in love. But he hadn't actually *said* he loved her.

She slanted her head, catching her lower lip between her teeth.

Ask him.

"Do you love me, Morgan?"

Well, it seemed she *did* have the cheeky boldness of a bloke with bull-sized ballocks, after all.

"My beautiful Scottish lass, I love you so much, my heart aches. My thoughts are consumed with you. And if I adore you this much after such a short period of time, spending decades with you will be such a blessing, I can hardly comprehend its magnitude."

She blinked away a sudden surge of joyful tears. "Aye, Morgan. Then, I'm sure."

He released a great, shuddery breath.

"Thank God. The hardest thing I've ever done was telling you to marry Sterling, when I wanted to claim you for my own. I love you, Shona, Lady Atterberry." He kissed her then, such reverence and adoration in the firm pressing of his lips upon hers that tears sprang to her eyes once more.

She opened to his gentle probing, pouring every ounce of her love into the tangling of their tongues.

It mattered naught if anyone else thought her too hasty. This incontestable pull, a meshing of spirits, as if they'd searched and searched, until they'd finally and instantly recognized their mates, could not be denied.

That was all that mattered.

Breathing heavily, Morgan at last levered away.

She was instantly bereft. Being in his arms was akin to coming home after an extended journey.

He kissed her forehead. "And you'll marry me?" A bit of hesitation still leached into his voice. "Not for several months, though. We don't want the gossips to have an apoplexy. It will give me time to court you properly."

"Several months?" Not a bit of it. Shona formed a *moue* with her mouth and shook her head as a pair of swans glided past. "I don't wish to wait."

"Three months then. I suppose I ought to be rather

flattered you're so eager to wed me." His wink was decidedly, and deliciously, as devilish as his grin. "Now, tell me. What did you wager Miss Rossington?"

"Why, that before week's end, I'd kiss the most attractive man here." She stood on her toes and wound her arms about his neck. "And I won that marvelously wicked wager."

Epilogue

Wedderford Abbey
January 29, 1821

Morgan traced a fingertip across Shona's collarbone.

Turning toward him, she smiled and sighed softly in her sleep.

This generous, sweet-natured, exquisite woman—a veritable wanton tigress in his bed—was his beloved wife. He glanced at the bedside clock.

Had been for thirteen months, two days, and twenty blissful hours.

Astonishingly, he grew to love her more with each passing day. And daily, often more than once, he sent a silent prayer of gratitude heavenward, not just for having her in his life, but that he'd been fuming in the oak stand that providential afternoon she'd tottered into the lake.

Had he not been there, she wouldn't be lying beside him, and they'd not be as happy and content as a colony of mice given full reign of the larder.

Once married, he'd insisted she permit him to take on the steward's role. Morgan hated idleness, but more importantly, he needed to contribute to their household. He'd brought no money to their marriage, so the least he could do was assist in running Wedderford Abbey.

The glow of Shona's ivory skin in the firelight proved irresistible.

He bent his head and feathered kisses from her shell-like ear, down the graceful column of her throat, to the glorious swell of her full breasts, barely concealed beneath the filmy peach nightgown she wore.

As always, she smelled of orange blossoms with a hint of musk.

"Morgan?" she murmured sleepily as he fingered the linen aside, affording him the luxury of the splendid display beneath.

"I'm sorry, I didn't mean to wake you, darling." Years of rising before dawn had proved a difficult habit to break, so, as he did every morning, he'd stoked the fire to make sure she awoke to a warm chamber.

Today her siren's call, the urge to hold her cocooned within his embrace, had lured him back underneath the coverlet.

That and two months of celibacy.

Six weeks ago, she'd given him a son.

A strapping lad with thick chestnut hair, blue eyes, and his grandsire's vocal cords. And who, by the miracle of his very existence, had persuaded Ruben Le Draco that perhaps selling his tropical holdings in exchange for a relationship with his son and grandson was a most fair bargain indeed. Father had even confessed he'd never removed Morgan from his will. For his part, Morgan had taken a wait-and-see approach to his sire's change of heart.

He scooted lower and tucked Shona into his side,

his groin pulsing with hot need.

Hounds' teeth, he wasn't a stag in the rut, a wild beast who'd fall upon his still recovering wife. Though, truth be told, despite the daily plunges into the frigid pond behind the manor—more of a smallish loch, actually—he'd limped about with a constant cockstand the past fortnight.

Shona draped her thigh across his, bumping the disgruntled appendage between his legs, and Morgan stiffened and groaned.

She nudged his penis again, and he swatted her wonderfully rounded bottom.

"Stop that, or I won't be responsible for what happens."

She giggled, and giving him a coy look, brushed her fingertips down his torso in a torturously slow descent.

Stomach muscles tense and his breath suspended, he prayed she'd venture lower still.

God, please.

"Mayhap I want *that* to happen." She slid her hand another pair of inches under the bed clothes. "The doctor said I might assume my wifely duties. Although," she encircled him with her soft hand, and Morgan reflexively bucked his hips upward, "I don't concur with his analysis."

Scorching disappointment battered him. Still, he summoned a smile and cupped her face. "When you're ready, my sweet."

"Oh, I'm ready. I've been ready for weeks, but was forbidden coitus. I referred to the doctor's flawed assumption that the more intimate parts of marriage are an obligation I must endure." She rose, and then, with a sultry half-smile, straddled him. "I quite like this part of married life."

"Indeed?" Morgan grinned and splayed his hands atop her thighs, slowly pushing her silky nightgown even higher.

Her full breasts, made more so since she insisted on nursing their son, swung tantalizingly close to his face beneath their wispy covering.

He'd suspected she possessed a fiery, sensual streak beneath her carefully subdued exterior.

He gritted his teeth, his raspy breath hissing from

between his teeth blending with her blissful gasp as she lowered herself onto him.

"I love you, Shona." He gripped her hips, letting her set the pace.

She smiled, rapture blooming across her radiant face. "I ken. And I love ye. We are proof that love at first sight truly exists."

"Indeed, we are."

About the Author

USA Today Bestselling, award-winning author COLLETTE CAMERON® scribbles Scottish and Regency historicals featuring dashing rogues and scoundrels and the intrepid damsels who re-form them. Blessed with an overactive and witty muse that won't stop whispering new romantic romps in her ear, she's lived in Oregon her entire life, though she dreams of living in Scotland part-time. A self-confessed Cadbury chocoholic, you'll always find a dash of inspiration and a pinch of humor in her sweet-to-spicy timeless romances®.

Explore **Collette's worlds** at
www.collettecameron.com!

Join her **VIP Reader Club** and **FREE newsletter**.
Giggles guaranteed!

FREE BOOK: Join Collette's The Regency Rose® VIP Reader Club to get updates on book releases, cover reveals, contests and giveaways she reserves exclusively for email and newsletter followers. Also, any deals, sales, or special promotions are offered to club members first. She will not share your name or email, nor will she spam you.

http://bit.ly/TheRegencyRoseGift

From the Desk of Collette Cameron

Dearest Reader,

I'm so thrilled you chose to read ***The Rogue and the Wallflower***. Since I introduced Shona Atterberry in ***Heartbreak and Honor,*** and mentioned her in ***To Capture a Rogue's Heart***, I thought she deserved her own story.

Though she was a victim, she refused to let her past shape her future. At first readers might think she's a weak, feckless character, but she proves she's not. I hope you grew to admire her as much as I did.

As for Morgan—such an inherently decent man deserved a woman to adore him, despite his scars. Shona sees him through the eyes of love, just as he sees her.

For those who might struggle with the love at first sight concept, or think the romance was rushed, I actually researched love at first sight and surveyed a slew of readers to see if the phenomenon exists. It does! My cousin's husband asked her to marry him on their first date, and reader after reader shared their delightfully romantic tales of immediate love and swift marriages that have lasted for decades.

Please consider telling other readers why you enjoyed this book by reviewing it. Not only do I truly want to hear your thoughts, reviews are crucial for an author to succeed. Even if you only leave a line or two, I'd very much appreciate it.

So, with that I'll leave you.

Here's wishing you many happy hours of reading, more happily ever afters than you can possibly enjoy in a lifetime, and abundant blessings to you and your loved-ones.

Collette Cameron

A Kiss for a Rogue
The Honorable Rogues®, Book One

Formerly titled A Kiss for Miss Kingsley

A lonely wallflower. A future viscount. A second chance at love.

Olivia Kingsley didn't expect to be swept off her feet and receive a marriage proposal two weeks into her first Season. However, one delicious dance with Allen Wimpleton, and her future is sealed. Or so she thinks until her eccentric father suddenly announces he's moving the family to the Caribbean for a year.

Terrified of losing Olivia, Allen begs her to elope, but she refuses. Distraught at her leaving, and unaware of her father's ill-health, Allen doubts her love and foolishly demands she choose—him or her father.

Heartbroken at his callousness, Olivia turns her back on their love. The year becomes three, enough time for her broken heart to heal, and after her father dies, she returns to England.

Coming face to face with Allen at a ball, she realizes she never purged him from her heart.

But can they overcome their pasts and old wounds to trust love again? Or has Allen found another in her absence?

Enjoy the first chapter of
A Kiss for a Rogue
The Honorable Rogues®, Book One

A lady must never forget her
manners nor lose her composure.
~*A Lady's Guide to Proper Comportment*

1

London, England
Late May, 1818

"This is a monumental mistake."

God's toenails. What were you thinking, Olivia Kingsley, agreeing to Auntie Muriel's addlepated scheme?

Why had she ever agreed to this farce?

Fingering the heavy ruby pendant hanging at the hollow of her neck, Olivia peeked out the window as the conveyance rounded the corner onto Berkeley Square. Good God. Carriage upon carriage, like great shiny beetles, lined the street beside an ostentatious manor. Her heart skipped a long beat, and she ducked out of sight.

Braving another glance from the window's corner, her stomach pitched worse than a ship amid a hurricane. The full moon's milky light, along with the mansion's rows of glowing diamond-shaped panes, illuminated the street. Dignified guests in their evening finery swarmed before the grand entrance and on the granite stairs as they waited their turn to enter Viscount and Viscountess Wimpleton's home.

The manor had acquired a new coat of paint since she had seen it last. She didn't care for the pale lead shade, preferring the previous color, a pleasant, welcoming bronze green. Why anyone living in Town would choose to wrap their home in such a chilly color was beyond her. With its enshrouding fog and perpetually overcast skies, London boasted every

A KISS FOR A ROGUE Excerpt

shade of gray already.

Three years in the tropics, surrounded by vibrant flowers, pristine powdery beaches, a turquoise sea, and balmy temperatures had rather spoiled her against London's grime and stench. How long before she grew accustomed to the dank again? The gloom? The smell?

Never.

Shivering, Olivia pulled her silk wrap snugger. Though late May, she'd been nigh on to freezing since the ship docked last week.

A few curious guests turned to peer in their carriage's direction. A lady swathed in gold silk and dripping diamonds, spoke into her companion's ear and pointed at the gleaming carriage. Did she suspect someone other than Aunt Muriel sat behind the distinctive Daventry crest?

Trepidation dried Olivia's mouth and tightened her chest. Would many of the *ton* remember her?

Stupid question, that. Of course she would be remembered.

Much like ivy—its vines clinging tenaciously to a tree—or a barnacle cemented to a rock, one couldn't easily be pried from the upper ten thousand's memory. But, more on point, would anyone recall her fascination with Allen Wimpleton?

Inevitably.

Coldness didn't cause the new shudder rippling from her shoulder to her waist.

Yes. Attending the ball was a featherbrained solicitation for disaster. No good could come of it. Flattening against the sky-blue and gold-trimmed velvet squab in the corner of her aunt's coach, Olivia vehemently shook her head.

"I cannot do it. I thought I could, but I positively cannot."

A curl came loose, plopping onto her forehead.

Bother.

The dratted, rebellious nuisance that passed for her hair escaped its confines more often than not. She shoved the annoying tendril beneath a pin, having no doubt the tress would work its way free again before evenings end. Patting the circlet of rubies adorning her hair, she assured herself the band remained secure. The treasure had belonged to Aunt Muriel's mother, a

A KISS FOR A ROGUE Excerpt

Prussian princess, and no harm must come to it.

Olivia's pulse beat an irregular staccato as she searched for a plausible excuse for refusing to attend the ball after all. She wouldn't lie outright, which ruled out her initial impulse to claim a *megrim*.

"I ... we—" She wiggled her white-gloved fingers at her brother, lounging on the opposite seat. "Were not invited."

Contented as their fat cat, Socrates, after lapping a saucer of fresh cream, Bradford settled his laughing gaze on her. "Yes, we mustn't do anything untoward."

Terribly vulgar, that. Arriving at a *haut ton* function, no invitation in hand. She and Bradford mightn't make it past the vigilant majordomo, and then what were they to do? Scuttle away like unwanted pests? Mortifying and prime tinder for the gossips.

"Whatever will people *think*?" Bradford thrived on upending Society. If permitted, he would dance naked as a robin just to see the reactions. He cocked a cinder-black brow, his gray-blue eyes holding a challenge.

Toad.

Olivia yearned to tell him to stop giving her that

loftier look. Instead, she bit her tongue to keep from sticking it out at him like she had as a child. Irrationality warred with reason, until her common sense finally prevailed. "I wouldn't want to impose, is all I meant."

"Nonsense, darling. It's perfectly acceptable for you and Bradford to accompany me." The seat creaked as Aunt Muriel, the Duchess of Daventry, bent forward to scrutinize the crowd. She patted Olivia's knee. "Lady Wimpleton is one of my dearest friends. Why, we had our come-out together, and I'm positive had she known that you and Bradford had recently returned to England, she would have extended an invitation herself."

Olivia pursed her lips.

Not if she knew the volatile way her son and I parted company, she wouldn't have.

A powerful peeress, few risked offending Aunt Muriel, and she knew it well. She could haul a haberdasher or a milkmaid to the ball and everyone would paste artificial smiles on their faces and bid the duo a pleasant welcome. Reversely, if someone earned her scorn, they had best pack-up and leave London permanently before doors began slamming in their faces. Her influence rivaled that of the Almack's patronesses.

Bradford shifted, presenting Olivia with his striking profile as he, too, took in the hubbub before the manor. "You will never be at peace—never be able to move on—unless you do this."

That morsel of knowledge hadn't escaped her, which was why she had agreed to the scheme to begin with. Nevertheless, that didn't make seeing Allen Wimpleton again any less nerve-wracking.

"You must go in, Livy," Bradford urged, his countenance now entirely brotherly concern.

She stopped plucking at her mantle and frowned. "Please don't call me that, Brady."

Once, a lifetime ago, Allen had affectionately called her Livy—until she had refused to succumb to his begging and run away to Scotland. Regret momentarily altered her heart rhythm.

Bradford hunched one of his broad shoulders and scratched his eyebrow. "What harm can come of it?

We'll only stay as long as you like, and I promise, I shall remain by your side the entire time."

Their aunt's unladylike snort echoed throughout the carriage.

"And the moon only shines in the summer." Her voice dry as desert sand, and skepticism peaking her eyebrows high on her forehead, Aunt Muriel fussed with her gloves. "Nephew, I have never known you to forsake an opportunity to become, er ..."

She slid Olivia a guarded glance. "Shall we say, become better acquainted with the ladies? This Season, there are several tempting beauties and a particularly large assortment of amiable young widows eager for a *distraction*."

Did Aunt Muriel truly believe Olivia don't know about Bradford's reputation with females? She was neither blind nor ignorant.

He turned and flashed their aunt one of his dazzling smiles, his deeply tanned face making it all the more brighter. "All pale in comparison to you two lovelies, no doubt."

Olivia made an impolite noise and, shaking her

head, aimed her eyes heavenward in disbelief.

Doing it much too brown. Again.

Bradford was too charming by far—one reason the fairer sex were drawn to him like ants to molasses. She'd been just as doe-eyed and vulnerable when it came to Allen.

"Tish tosh, young scamp. Your compliments are wasted on me." Still, Aunt Muriel slanted her head, a pleased smile hovered on her lightly-painted mouth and pleating the corners of her eyes. "Besides, if you attach yourself to your sister, she won't have an opportunity to find herself alone with young Wimpleton."

Olivia managed to keep her jaw from unhinging as she gaped at her aunt. She snapped her slack mouth shut with an audible click. "Shouldn't you be cautioning me *not* to be alone with a gentleman?"

Aunt Muriel chuckled and patted Olivia's knee again. "That rather defeats the purpose in coming tonight then, doesn't it, dear?" Giving a naughty wink, she nudged Olivia. "I do hope Wimpleton kisses you. He's such a handsome young man. Quite the

Corinthian too."

A hearty guffaw escaped Bradford, and he slapped his knee. "Aunt Muriel, I refuse to marry until I find a female as colorful as you. Life would never be dull."

"I should say not. Daventry and I had quite the adventurous life. It's in my blood, you know, and yours too, I suspect. Papa rode his stallion right into a church and actually snatched Mama onto his lap moments before she was forced to marry an abusive lecher. The scandal, they say, was utterly delicious." The duchess sniffed, a put-upon expression on her lined face. "Dull indeed. *Hmph*. Never. Why, I may have to be vexed with you the entire evening for even hinting such a preposterous thing."

"Grandpapa abducted Grandmamma? In church, no less?" Bradford dissolved into another round of hearty laughter, something he did often as evidenced by the lines near his eyes.

Unable to utter a single sensible rebuttal, Olivia swung her gaze between them. Her aunt and brother beamed, rather like two naughty imps, not at all abashed at having been caught with their mouth's full of stolen sweetmeats from the kitchen.

She wrinkled her nose and gave a dismissive flick of her wrist. "Bah. You two are completely hopeless where decorum is concerned."

"Don't mistake decorum for stodginess or pomposity, my dear." Her aunt gave a sage nod. "Neither permits a mite of fun and both make one a cantankerous boor."

Bradford snickered again, his hair, slightly too long for London, brushing his collar. "By God, if only there were more women like you."

Olivia itched to box his ears. Did he take nothing seriously?

No. Not since Philomena had died.

Olivia edged near the window once more and worried the flesh of her lower lip. Carriages continued to line up, two or three abreast. Had the entire *beau monde* turned out for the grand affair?

Botheration. Why must the Wimpletons be so well-received?

She caught site of her tense face reflected in the glass, and hastily turned away.

"And, Aunt Muriel, you're absolutely positive that Allen—that is, Mr. Wimpleton—remains unattached?"

Fiddling with her shawl's silk fringes, Olivia attempted a calming breath. No force on heaven or earth could compel her to enter the manor if Allen were betrothed or married to another. Her fragile heart, though finally mended after three years of painful healing, could bear no more anguish or regret.

If he were pledged to another, she would simply take the carriage back to Aunt Muriel's, pack her belongings, and make for Bromham Hall, Bradford's newly inherited country estate. Olivia would make a fine spinster; perhaps even take on the task of housekeeper in order to be of some use to her brother. She would never set foot in Town again.

She dashed her aunt an impatient, sidelong peek. Why didn't Aunt Muriel answer the question?

Head to the side and eyes brimming with compassion, Aunt Muriel regarded her.

"You're certain he's not courting anyone?" Olivia pressed for the truth. "There's no one he has paid marked attention to? You must tell me, mustn't fear for

A KISS FOR A ROGUE Excerpt

my sensibilities or that I'll make a scene."

She didn't make scenes.

The *A Lady's Guide to Proper Comportment* was most emphatic in that regard.

Only the most vulgar and lowly bred indulge in histrionics or emotional displays.

Aunt Muriel shook her turbaned head firmly. The bold ostrich feather topping the hair covering jolted violently, and her diamond and emerald cushion-shaped earrings swung with the force of her movement. She adjusted her gaudily-colored shawl.

"No. No one. Not from the lack of enthusiastic mamas, and an audacious papa or two, shoving their simpering daughters beneath his nose, I can tell you. Wimpleton's considered a brilliant catch, quite dashing, and a top-sawyer, to boot." She winked wickedly again. "Why, if I were only a score of years younger ..."

"Yes? What *would* you do, Aunt Muriel?" Rubbing his jaw, Bradford grinned.

Olivia flung him a flinty-eyed glare. "Hush. Do not encourage her."

Worse than children, the two of them.

Lips pursed, Aunt Muriel ceased fussing with her skewed pendant and tapped her fingers upon her plump thigh. "I would wager a year's worth of my favorite pastries that fast Rossington chit has set her cap for him, though. Has her feline claws dug in deep, too, I fear."

A Bride for a Rogue

The Honorable Rogues®, Book Two

Formerly titled Bride of Falcon

She can't forget the past. He can't face the future. Until fate intervenes one night.

Many years ago, Ivonne Wimpleton loved Chancy Faulkenhurst and hoped to marry him. Then one day, without any explanation, he sailed to India. Now, after five unsuccessful Seasons and a riding accident that left her with a slight limp, her only suitors are fortune-hunters and degenerates. Just as Ivy's resigned herself to spinsterhood, Chance unexpectedly returns.

Upon returning to England, Chance is disillusioned, disfigured, and emotionally scarred, but his love for Ivy remains is strong. However, he's failed to acquire the fortune he sought in order to earn permission to marry her. When he discovers Ivy's being forced to wed to prevent a scandalous secret from being revealed, he's determined to make her his bride.

Except, believing Chance made no effort to contact her all those years, Ivy's furious with him. What's more, in his absence, his father arranged a profitable marriage for Chance. As he battles his own inner demons, he must convince Ivy to risk loving him again. But will their parents' interference jeopardize Chance and Ivy's happiness once more?

A Rogue's Scandalous Wish
The Honorable Rogues®, Book Three

Formerly titled Her Scandalous Wish

A marriage offered out of obligation…

…an acceptance compelled by desperation.

At the urging of her dying brother, Philomena Pomfrett reluctantly agrees to attend a London Season. If she fails to acquire a husband, her future is perilous. Betrayed once by Bradford, Viscount Kingsley, as well as scarred from a horrific fire, Philomena entertains no notions of a love-match. Hers will be a marriage of convenience. *If* she can find man who will have her.

When the woman he loves dies, Bradford leaves England and its painful memories behind. After a three-year absence, he returns home but doesn't recognize his first love when he stumbles upon her hiding in a shadowy arbor during a ball. Something about the mysterious woman enthralls him, and he steals a moonlit kiss. Caught in the act by Philomena's brother, Bradford is issued an ultimatum—a duel or marry her.

Bradford refuses to duel with a gravely-ill man and offers marriage. But Philomena rejects his half-hearted proposal, convinced he'd grow to despise her when he sees her disfiguring scars. Then her brother collapses, and frantic to provide the medical care he needs, she's faced with marrying a man who deserted her once already.

To Capture a Rogue's Heart

The Honorable Rogues®, Book Four

Formerly titled To Tame a Scoundrel's Heart

He recruited her to help him find a wife…

…and discovered she was the perfect candidate.

Her betrothed cheated on her.
Katrina Needham intended to marry her beloved major and live happily-ever-after—until he's seen with another woman. Distraught, and needing a distraction, she agrees to assist the rugged, and dangerously handsome Captain Dominic St. Monté find a wife. So why does she find herself entertaining romantic notions about the privateer turned duke?

He believed he was illegitimate.
When Nic unexpectedly inherits a dukedom and the care of his young sisters, he reluctantly decides he must marry. Afterward, if his new duchess is willing, he hopes to return to the sea-faring life he craves part-time. If she doesn't agree, he'll have no choice but to give up the sea forever.

Will they forsake everything for each other?
Nic soon realizes Katrina possesses every characteristic he seeks in a duchess. The more time he spends with the vivacious beauty, the more enamored he becomes. Still, he cannot ask for her hand. Not only is she still officially promised to another, she has absolutely no interest in becoming a duchess, much less a privateer's wife.

Can Nic and Katrina relinquish their carefully planned futures and trust love to guide them?

The Earl and the Spinster

The Blue Rose Regency Romances:
The Culpepper Misses, Book One

Formerly titled Brooke: Wagers Gone Awry

An angry earl. A desperate spinster. A reckless wager.

For five years, Brooke Culpepper has focused her energy on two things: keeping the struggling dairy farm that's her home operating and preventing her younger sister and cousins from starving. Then one day, a stern-faced stranger arrives at their doorstep and announces he's the dairy's new owner and plans on selling the farm. Though she's outraged, Brooke can't deny the Earl of Ravensdale makes her pulse race in the most disturbing way.

Heath is incensed to discover five women call the land he won at the gaming tables their home. He detests everything about the country and has no desire to own a smelly farm, even if one of the occupants is the most intelligent, entrancing woman he's ever met.

Desperate, pauper poor, and with nowhere to take her family, Brooke rashly proposes a wager. Heath's stakes? The farm. Hers? Her virtue. The land holds no interest for Heath, but he finds Brooke irresistible, and ignoring prudence as well as his sense of honor, he just as recklessly accepts her challenge.

In a winner-takes-all bet, will they both come to regret their impulsiveness, especially when love is at stake?

Excerpt

Enjoy the first chapter of
The Earl and the Spinster
The Blue Rose Regency Romances:
The Culpepper Misses, Book One

Even when most prudently considered,
and with the noblest of intentions, one who
wagers with chance oft finds oneself empty-handed.
~*Wisdom and Advice*
The Genteel Lady's Guide to Practical Living

1

Esherton Green,
Near Acton, Cheshire, England
Early April 1822

Was I born under an evil star or cursed from my first breath?

Brooke Culpepper suppressed the urge to shake her fist at the heavens and berate The Almighty aloud.

The devil boasted better luck than she. My God, now two *more* cows struggled to regain their strength?

She slid Richard Mabry, Esherton Green's steward-turned-overseer, a worried glance from beneath her lashes as she chewed her lower lip and paced before the unsatisfactory fire in the study's hearth. The soothing aroma of wood smoke, combined with linseed oil, old leather, and the faintest trace of Papa's pipe tobacco, bathed the room. The scents reminded her of happier times but did little to calm her frayed nerves.

Sensible gray woolen skirts swishing about her ankles, she whirled to make the return trip across the once-bright green and gold Axminster carpet, now so threadbare, the oak floor peeked through in numerous places. Her scuffed half-boots fared little better, and she hid a wince when the scrap of leather she'd used to cover the hole in her left sole this morning slipped loose again.

From his comfortable spot in a worn and faded wingback chair, Freddy, her aged Welsh corgi, observed her progress with soulful brown eyes, his muzzle propped on stubby paws. Two ancient tabbies lay curled so tightly together on the cracked leather sofa that determining where one ended and the other began was difficult.

THE EARL AND THE SPINSTER Excerpt

What was she to do? Brooke clamped her lip harder and winced.

Should she venture to the barn to see the cows herself?

What good would that do? She knew little of doctoring cattle and so left the animals' care in Mr. Mabry's capable hands. Her strength lay in the financial administration of the dairy farm and her ability to stretch a shilling as thin as gossamer.

She cast a glance at the bay window and, despite the fire, rubbed her arms against the chill creeping along her spine. A frenzied wind whipped the lilac branches and scraped the rain-splattered panes. The tempest threatening since dawn had finally unleashed its full fury, and the fierce winds battering the house gave the day a peculiar, eerie feeling—as if portending something ominous.

At least Mabry and the other hands had managed to get the cattle tucked away before the gale hit. The herd of fifty—no, sixty, counting the newborn calves—chewed their cud and weathered the storm inside the old, but sturdy, barns.

As she peered through the blurry pane, a shingle ripped loose from the farthest outbuilding—a retired stone dovecote. After the wind tossed the slat around for a few moments, the wood twirled to the ground, where it flipped end over end before wedging beneath a gangly shrub. Two more shingles hurled to the earth, this time from one of the barns.

Flimflam and goose-butt feathers.

Brooke tamped down a heavy sigh. Each structure on the estate, including the house, needed some sort of repair or replacement: roofs, shutters, stalls, floors, stairs, doors, siding...dozens of items required fixing, and she could seldom muster the funds to go about it properly.

"Another pair of cows struggling, you say, Mr. Mabry?"

Concern etched on his weathered features, Mabry wiped rain droplets from his face as water pooled at his muddy feet.

"Yes, Miss Brooke. The four calves born this mornin' fare well, but two of the cows, one a first-calf heifer, aren't standin' yet. And there's one weak from birthin' her calf yesterday." His troubled gaze strayed to the window. "Two more ladies are in labor. I best return to the barn. They seemed fine when I left, but I'd as soon be nearby."

Brooke nodded once. "Yes, we mustn't take any chances."

The herd had already been reduced to a minimum by disease and sales to make ends meet. She needed every shilling the cows' milk brought. Losing another, let alone two or three good breeders...

No, I won't think of it.

She stopped pacing and forced a cheerful smile. Nonetheless, from the skeptical look Mabry speedily masked, his thoughts ran parallel to hers—one reason she put her trust in the man. Honest and intelligent, he'd worked alongside her to restore the beleaguered herd and farm after Papa died. Their existence, their livelihood, everyone at Esherton's future depended on the estate flourishing once more.

"It's only been a few hours." *Almost nine, truth to tell.* Brooke scratched her temple. "Perhaps the ladies need a little more time to recover." *If they recovered.* "The calves are strong, aren't they?" *Please, God, they must be.* She held her breath, anticipating Mabry's response.

His countenance lightened and the merry sparkle returned to his eyes. "Aye, the mites are fine. Feedin' like they're hollow to their wee hooves."

Tension lessoned its ruthless grip, and hope peeked from beneath her vast mound of worries.

Six calves had been guaranteed in trade to her neighbor and fellow dairy farmer, Silas Huffington, for the grain and medicines he'd provided to see Esherton Green's herd through last winter. Brooke didn't have the means to pay him if the calves didn't survive—though the old reprobate had hinted he'd make her a deal of a much less respectable nature if she ran short of cattle with which to barter. Each pence she'd stashed away—groat by miserable groat, these past four years—lay in the hidden drawer of Papa's desk and must go to purchase a bull.

Wisdom had decreed replacing Old Buford two years ago but, short on funds, she'd waited until it was too late. His heart had stopped while he performed the duties expected of a breeding bull. Not the worst way to cock up one's toes...er, hooves, but she'd counted on him siring at least two-score calves this season and wagered everything on the calving this year and next. The poor brute had expired before he'd completed the job.

Her thoughts careened around inside her skull. Without a bull, she would lose everything.

My home, care of my sister and cousins, my reasons for existing.

She squared her shoulders, resolution strengthening her. She still retained the Culpepper sapphire parure set. If all else failed, she would pawn the jewelry. She'd planned on using the money from the gems' sale to bestow small marriage settlements on the girls. Still, pawning the set was a price worth paying to keep her family at Esherton Green, even if it meant that any chance of her sister and three cousins securing a decent match would evaporate faster than a dab of milk on a hot cook stove. Good standing and breeding meant little if one's fortune proved meaner than a churchyard beggar's.

"How's the big bull calf that came breech on Sunday?" Brooke tossed the question over her shoulder as she poked the fire and encouraged the blaze to burn hotter. After setting the tool aside, she faced the overseer.

"Greediest of the lot." Mabry laughed and slapped his thigh. "Quite the appetite he has, and friendly as our Freddy there. Likes his ears scratched too."

Brooke chuckled and ran her hand across Freddy's spine. The dog wiggled in excitement and stuck his rear legs straight out behind him, gazing at her in adoration. In his youth, he'd been an excellent cattle herder. Now he'd gone fat and arthritic, his sweet face gray to his eyebrows. On occasion, he still dashed after the cattle, the instinctive drive to herd deep in the marrow of his bones.

Another shudder shook her. Why was she so blasted cold today? She relented and placed a good-sized log atop the others. The feeble flames hissed and spat before greedily engulfing the new addition. Lord, she prayed she wasn't ailing. She simply couldn't afford to become ill.

A scratching at the door barely preceded the entrance of Duffen bearing a tea service. "Gotten to where a man cannot find a quiet corner to shut his eyes for a blink or two anymore."

Shuffling into the room, he yawned and revealed how few teeth remained in his mouth. One sock sagged around his ankle, his grizzled hair poked every which way, and his shirttail hung askew. Typical Duffen.

"Devil's day, it is." He scowled in the window's direction, his mouth pressed into a grim line. "Mark my words, trouble's afoot."

Not quite a butler, but certainly more than a simple retainer, the man, now hunched from age, had been a fixture at Esherton Green Brooke's entire life. He loved the place as much as, if not more than, she, and she couldn't afford to hire a servant to replace him. A light purse had forced Brooke to let the household staff go when Papa died. The cook, Mrs. Jennings, Duffen, and Flora, a maid-of-all-work, had stayed on. However, they received no salaries—only room and board.

The income from the dairy scarcely permitted Brooke to retain a few milkmaids and stable hands, yet not once had she heard a whispered complaint from anyone.

Everybody, including Brooke, her sister, Brette, and their cousins—Blythe, and the twins, Blaike and Blaire—did their part to keep the farm operating at a profit. A meager profit, particularly as, for the past five years, Esherton Green's legal heir, Sheridan Gainsborough, had received half the proceeds. In return, he permitted Brooke and the girls to reside there. He'd also been appointed their guardian. But, from his silence and failure to visit the farm, he seemed perfectly content to let her carry on as provider and caretaker.

"Ridiculous law. Only the next male in line can inherit," she muttered.

Especially when he proved a disinterested bore. Papa had thought so too, but the choice hadn't been his to make. If only she could keep the funds she sent to Sheridan each quarter, Brooke could make something of Esherton and secure her sister and cousins' futures too.

If wishes were gold pieces, I'd be rich indeed.

Brooke sneezed then sneezed again. Dash it all. A cold?

The fresh log snapped loudly, and Brooke started. The blaze's heat had failed to warm her opinion of her second cousin. She hadn't met him and lacked a personal notion of his character, but Papa had hinted that Sheridan was a scallywag and possessed unsavory habits.

A greedy sot, too.

The one time her quarterly remittance had been late, because Brooke had taken a tumble and broken her arm, he'd written a disagreeable letter demanding his money.

His money, indeed.

Sheridan had threatened to sell Esherton Green's acreage and turn her and the foursome onto the street if she ever delayed payment again.

A ruckus beyond the entrance announced the girls' arrival. Laughing and chatting, the blond quartet billowed into the room. Their gowns, several seasons out of fashion, in no way detracted from their charm, and pride swelled in Brooke's heart. Lovely, both in countenance and disposition, and the dears worked hard too.

"Duffen says we're to have tea in here today." Attired in a Pomona green gown too short for her tall frame, Blaike plopped on to the sofa. Her twin, Blaire, wearing a similar dress in dark rose and equally inadequate in length, flopped beside her.

Each girl scooped a drowsy cat into her lap. The cats' wiry whiskers twitched, and they blinked their sleepy amber eyes a few times before closing them once more as the low rumble of contented purrs filled the room.

"Yes, I didn't think we needed to light a fire in the drawing room when this one will suffice." As things stood, too little coal and seasoned firewood remained to see them comfortably until summer.

Brette sailed across the study, her slate-blue gingham dress the only one of the quartet's fashionably long enough. Repeated laundering had turned the garment a peculiar greenish color, much like tarnished copper. She looped her arm through Brooke's.

"Look, dearest." Brette pointed to the tray. "I splurged and made a half-batch of shortbread biscuits. It's been so long since we've indulged, and today is your birthday. To celebrate, I insisted on fresh tea leaves as well."

Brooke would have preferred to ignore the day.

Three and twenty.

On the shelf. Past her prime. Long in the tooth. Spinster. *Old maid.*

She'd relinquished her one chance at love. In order to nurse her ailing father and assume the care of her young sister and three orphaned cousins, she'd refused Humphrey Benbridge's proposal. She couldn't have put her happiness before their welfare and deserted them when they needed her most. Who would've cared for them if she hadn't?

No one.

Mr. Benbridge controlled the purse strings, and Humphrey had neither offered nor been in a position to take on their care. Devastated, or so he'd claimed, he'd departed to the continent five years ago.

She'd not seen him since.

Nonetheless, his sister, Josephina, remained a friend and occasionally remarked on Humphrey's travels abroad. Burying the pieces of her broken heart beneath hard work and devotion to her family, Brooke had rolled up her sleeves and plunged into her forced role as breadwinner, determined that sacrificing her love not be in vain.

Yes, it grieved her that she wouldn't experience a man's passion or bear children, but to wallow in doldrums was a waste of energy and emotion. Instead, she focused on building a future for her sister and cousins—so they might have what she never would—and allowed her dreams to fade into obscurity.

"Happy birthday." Brette squeezed her hand.

Brooke offered her sister a rueful half-smile. "Ah, I'd hoped you'd forgotten."

"Don't be silly, Brooke. We couldn't forget your

THE EARL AND THE SPINSTER Excerpt

special day." Twenty-year-old Blythe—standing with her hands behind her—grinned and pulled a small, neatly-wrapped gift tied with a cheerful yellow ribbon from behind her. Sweet dear. She'd used the trimming from her gown to adorn the package.

"Hmph. Need seedcake an' champagne to celebrate a birthday properly." The contents of the tray rattled and clanked when Duffen scuffed his way to the table between the sofa and chairs. After depositing the tea service, he lifted a letter from the surface. Tea dripped from one stained corner. "This arrived for you yesterday, Miss Brooke. I forgot where I'd put it until just now."

If I can read it with the ink running to London and back.

He shook the letter, oblivious to the tawny droplets spraying every which way.

Mabry raised a bushy gray eyebrow, and the twins hid giggles by concealing their faces in the cat's striped coats.

Brette set about pouring the tea, although her lips twitched suspiciously.

Freddy sat on his haunches and barked, his button eyes fixed on the paper, evidently mistaking it for a tasty morsel he would've liked to sample. He licked his chops, a testament to his waning eyesight.

"Thank you, Duffen." Brooke took the letter by one soggy corner. Holding it gingerly, she flipped it over. No return address.

"Aren't you going to read it?" Blythe set the gift on the table before settling on the sofa and smoothing her skirt. They didn't get a whole lot of post at Esherton. Truth be known, this was the first letter in months. Blythe's gaze roved to the other girls and the equally eager expressions on their faces. "We're on pins and needles," she quipped, fluttering her hands and winking.

Brooke smiled and cracked the brownish wax seal with her fingernail. Their lives had become rather monotonous, so much so that a simple, *soggy*, correspondence sent the girls into a dither of anticipation.

My Dearest Cousin...

Brooke glanced up. "It's from Sheridan.

Printed in Great Britain
by Amazon